WILLIAM

CLYDE SUTTON

WILLIAM

CLYDE SUTTON

LIVING TREES PRESS

Living Trees Press
43 Waimaunga Road
RD 2
Raglan 3296
New Zealand

First published by Köehler Books 2015
This edition published by Living Trees Press 2018
© Copyright 2017, 2018 Clyde Sutton

ISBN 978-0-473-48145-2

A catalogue record for this book is available from the National Library of New Zealand.

Design and layout of text: PressGang www.pressgang.co.nz
Design of cover: Köehler Books
Printed in China by Asia Pacific Offset

TO ALL THOSE WHO CHOOSE PEACE

– CHAPTER 1 –

CONFUSION

WILLIAM GLANCED at the wall.

"All you need to do is see your body as invulnerable, much stronger than any steel." And then he just walked right through the concrete wall of the building. Like it was the most normal thing in the world. You can imagine the effect that had on all the government observers and scientists assembled in that secret room assuming they were there to expose another fake.

William smiled as he stepped back through the ragged hole before the dust settled. Light shone around him from the sunny day outside and the sparkles from the floating dust created an eerie effect for the people in the gloomy room.

"The time you kindly allowed me for my lecture and demonstration is well over so when you have some more questions for me, you know where to contact me," William said before he walked out of the room—except by the door this time.

Of the many memories William shared with me that was one he particularly treasured; he recalled happily the shocked look on the faces of all those dour experts and scientists as he stepped back into the room. They had come face to face with something alien to their world view and, deep down, they stubbornly refused to admit it was possible despite having seen William walk through a wall with their own eyes. He had shattered their secure little view of the world.

I first met William in Los Angeles after spending the day wasting time at Disneyland, doing all those touristy things. I walked out of the park and got on the bus from Disneyland to Anaheim, where I was staying at a motel for a few days.

This guy was one of a group of people who got on the bus at a later stop. He looked kind of unkempt with wild hair and beard as he stood gazing down the aisle, so I went back to staring out the window and ignored him. There were lots of empty seats, but after a while he slowly walked down and, after putting his backpack on the seat in front, sat down beside me with a big smile showing through his beard. I was more than a bit nervous, as I was travelling alone and there was nobody sitting near me.

He gave me a hug while I tried to shrink back, which is not easy when you are squashed against the window in a bus seat. When his face was beside my ear he whispered, "Please play along, I'm really sorry about this" and then gently kissed my lips. Oddly enough, my strongest thought was that I don't like bushy beards.

He started talking happily as the bus moved off, peppering me with questions about how my day was going and what I was doing on the bus. When he stopped for a breath I just stared back at him and then said quietly, "If you don't tell me what's going on here I am going to start screaming."

He paused briefly and seemed to go kind of blank. After an eerie few moments he said, "I can tell you are trustworthy and I don't know why but it seems important that I tell you the truth. Will you promise not to tell anybody about me or alert the police if I tell you why I sat here?"

All I said was, "Okay," while thinking this had better be good.

"First of all," he said, "I am on the run trying to hide from the government, or rather a clandestine part of it." He saw the look on my face and quickly added, "But don't worry, I'm not a threat to you. I have not done anything criminal, other than being different.

"To their way of thinking that is enough to make me a threat and require that I either be under their control or eliminated. Two men were chasing me earlier and another two who I am sure are also working with them drove by while I was sitting at the stop. Agents have been alerted to look out for men fitting my description, and while I don't know if there were agents watching or not, I prefer not to take the chance. I got on the bus and came to sit by you as we are obviously fairly close in age. Making it look as if we are close friends or lovers does not fit my profile and should make them think I am not the man they are looking for."

I noticed he was turning his head and looking behind regularly while he was telling me this. He sat silently for a time, still looking around occasionally, finally relaxing.

"It looks like they are not following me."

As the bus approached another stop a few minutes later, he signaled the driver that he wanted to get off. When the bus was pulling over he said, "Goodbye," and stood up to retrieve his pack from the seat in front. Feeling irritated by his casual dismissal I blurted out, "But you didn't even tell me your name." He just smiled, walked down the aisle and got off. I watched him walk down the street until he was out of sight, feeling both angry with him and disappointed that he never once looked back.

It is unusual for me to let other people get under my skin, but the oddness of the encounter kept the memory returning to plague me. I replayed the conversation over and over again in my head, trying to figure out if he had been for real or just some weirdo having fun at my expense. The problem with me is once something excites my curiosity, I just can't let it go.

* * * * *

I went on the Universal Pictures day tour the next day but didn't really enjoy myself as I spent most of the time feeling angry with somebody I didn't even know. About the only thing that cheered me up were the Jurassic Park and Revenge of the Mummy rides, which brought back happy memories of when I had seen the movies with friends from the technical institute where I had trained.

The following morning, I got up early to catch the bus to Las Vegas, feeling good because I was on the move again and getting out of LA. I'm not interested in taking bus tours to look at the houses of actors or Pamela Anderson's star on Broadway or other idiot touristy activities. *God, people, will you get a life or something?*

I love travelling and doing new things, the more challenging the better. Seeing the Grand Canyon has always been on my to-do list, and I was enjoying the rush of anticipation at fulfilling a long-held dream.

As the Greyhound pulled into a service center on the way to Las Vegas I saw him standing where the out lane left for the highway. He was obviously trying to hitch a ride. I got off the bus following the other passengers toward the diner; then on impulse, I turned around, bumping into the old lady behind me when she couldn't stop in time. After my apologies, I walked slowly up behind him, looking at him carefully.

He was slouching slightly, looking relaxed or maybe resigned—someone your eyes pass over without ever really noticing. He definitely was travelling light, wearing the same clothes he had been wearing in LA—well-worn and faded like his pack, but they had been freshly washed. It's amazing the amount of information you can get in a glance.

God, why am I even thinking like this? He is almost certainly paranoid and delusional but at least I know he doesn't need his mum to do his washing for him.

At a whim I said loudly—and as deeply as I could—"This is the police, hold it right..." His transformation was startling and incredible. He spun around with his fists clenched while adopting some kind of martial arts stance. The slightly disheveled or pathetic look was gone. There was no doubt he was a fighter and had reacted instinctively. He scared me enough to make me step back a pace or two. He was looking around and over my head for the real threat, having sized me up, instantly dismissing me before really noticing me.

His gaze finally settled on me as realization dawned and he snarled, "You are that girl from the bus in Los Angeles, aren't you? What the hell do you think you are doing?" I could feel the anger radiating from him.

I guess if I had thought things through a little more I should have expected this sort of reaction and would have handled things differently, but I tend to be a bit impulsive. Feeling angry at myself now as well him I said, "Look, it was only a joke, forget it," and started walking back to the diner.

After a few moments of indecision, he grabbed his pack and followed me. By the time he caught up we were at the door. He stopped me with a light touch on my shoulder saying, "Can we talk for a minute?"

"I don't have much time before the bus goes so you can come in and talk to me while I have something to eat if you want to."

He looked around, sighed and then said, "All right."

I realize, with the benefit of hindsight, that he only followed me back because of his intense sense of honor. He had yelled at me and felt he needed to explain and apologize, which overcame his usual reserve and caution. If I had walked up to him and spoken politely to him, he would have been polite to me too but would have ignored me at any deeper level and then moved on.

We chose a table and he sat with his pack at his feet while I walked over to the counter. At home they have a saying, "Real men don't eat quiche," so I ordered a slice of quiche and salad with a glass of milk for him while getting pancakes with maple syrup and a large mug of coffee for myself.

When I sat down in front of him he spoke straightaway.

"I'm sorry I shouted at you, but as you might understand I am a bit on edge at the moment."

"As I'm not supposed to talk to strange men you can tell me your name before going any further."

"I'm William, if that makes any difference. I might still be strange, in fact I can guarantee I am. I would just like to apologize and get out of here."

"I'm sorry too. I didn't mean to upset you out there." He started to get up and I put a hand on his saying, "Just sit awhile, you look as if you could do with it."

We sat at the table with an uneasy silence between us. When the waitress came with the order and started putting the pancakes in front of William I gleefully told her they were for me along with the coffee. I had intended to tease him a little about the food, but he just said, "Thank you," and ate it all, including the salad, even emptying the glass of milk. Watching him eat I realized he had been very hungry and had probably not eaten for a while. I was now feeling really guilty for being spiteful when he obviously was suffering. He said quietly as he finished, "When you do something odd like this it makes me memorable, and I prefer to avoid that, but thank you anyway."

As he got up to leave an Army Jeep drove slowly into the parking lot outside the window, and William sat again. I could see he was not going to say anything more, so I gestured in the direction of the Jeep and raised my eyebrows waiting for an answer.

"Part of what makes it so difficult is I never know who has been alerted to look for me. If they know I am in an area, they will send the local sheriff's department and other law enforcement agencies 'Wanted' posters with my picture. Usually though, the locals don't know I exist, but as I said before I can't afford to take the chance."

"I keep hearing *they*. Who are *they*, William?"

"I have been on the run for nearly twelve months now and they are never that far behind me. If I was a killer or hardened criminal, they would not care nearly as much. I wouldn't be worth the trouble of this continued high-level search. There are thousands of criminals, even murderers who never get caught, and the authorities never lose any sleep over it. I'm something far worse. I'm a threat to the established system that gives them their power. They can never tolerate something like that."

The Jeep had disappeared around the side of the building.

"Good. Looks like they left," William said, visibly relieved.

"Who are *they*?" I asked again.

"Ah," he answered thoughtfully. "The Military Police and Military Intelligence, probably Homeland Security, some other covert government agencies too I suspect. I am a deserter from the Army. They say I killed two men when I escaped their prison and went AWOL, but that's a lie they made up to justify the resources they are putting in to track me down. It helps them get assistance from civilian law enforcement agencies."

William rose from his seat to leave again. Just as he stood, the two soldiers who had been in the Jeep walked in the door.

"Shit, Rangers," William said under his breath as he dropped back into his seat.

"What's wrong with that?"

"I spent three years in the Rangers before I had to run. We are proud of what we do, the especially dangerous or difficult missions. We really hate deserters as it disgraces the honor and courage of our units."

"We?"

William just frowned, but I could see how much it hurt him to be considered a coward and dishonorable.

The soldiers sat at a table near us and looked around the diner as they talked, joked and waited for their meals to arrive. One of them, a sergeant I think, was staring at William from time to time but their meals arrived so they started eating. William had noticed this too.

"Excuse me a moment." He picked up his pack and walked slowly over to the corridor that led to the bathrooms and disappeared down it.

After a few more minutes I looked at my watch and knew I needed to get back to the bus soon. As I stepped out onto the pavement a strong hand took my arm at the elbow and propelled me around the side of the building. When we rounded another corner, I saw the Jeep parked close to the back wall of the building, taking advantage of the scant shade from the afternoon desert sun.

"Miss, I would like you to come with me and answer a few questions about the man you were with," the sergeant said.

The other soldier ran around the corner.

"You were right, he isn't in the bathroom."

The sergeant barked back, "Did you search the other rooms off the rest of the corridor? I did not see him out here, so he must be in there somewhere, get back and look properly."

The sergeant then turned back to me and said, "I have to report this, then we will have a nice little chat."

I could see the rear fire exit door was opening behind the sergeant as he fished in his pocket with his spare hand for the keys, obstinately refusing to let go of my arm. While he was still unlocking the door, William stepped silently up behind him and hit him on the back of his head. The sergeant crumpled slowly to the ground, releasing my arm as he fell.

William was already on his way back to the door. He almost stepped through, jerked to a stop and stepped behind it. A few moments later the other soldier emerged through the door heading back toward the sergeant. He stopped when he saw the sergeant at my feet, and at that moment

William hit him from behind too.

I was too shocked to move, but William had caught the soldier before he hit the ground and was half dragging, half carrying him to the back of the Jeep. He put him down to get the keys that were still in the front door to unlock the back door. He never paused, but said to me, "Did you tell them your name?"

"No, why?"

"How did you pay for your ticket—bank or credit cards?" When I looked blank he snapped, "For the bus, obviously."

"Neither, I paid cash."

"Great, in that case they have no record of you, but they will get a description of you when these men are found. I'll see to it that won't be for a while. You can get back on the bus and decide what you should do later."

I took that to mean he had not actually killed the men.

"Just don't draw attention to yourself."

Not liking to be ordered around I said, somewhat petulantly, "What happens if I stay?"

"In that case, if you have any luggage on the bus that identifies you, they will find out who you are when it is not claimed."

He continued. "On the bus in LA I was just using you as camouflage—protective coloration to make me blend in with everyday activities and not stand out as much. But I really did not mean to involve you with my problems. I'm sorry I did that now. If you are linked to me your own life will be in danger too as they don't know how much I have told you. They won't care if they decide to kill you anyway. After all, killing people is what the military does best."

I gave him the name of the hotel I would be staying at in Las Vegas.

He lifted his eyebrows. "It was in my price bracket, all right?" I said in my defense. "Meet me there and let me understand what this is all about, please."

He only nodded, so I said, "Promise me, word of honor."

"On my word I will be there, I have an obligation to you now. Now get out of here!"

He was already struggling to fit the sergeant into the back.

"Ask for Diane," I called as I ran for my bus.

CHAPTER 2

LAS VEGAS

I MADE IT TO THE BUS just as the driver was about to close the doors and tried not to gasp as I walked to my seat. Thoughts were tumbling over each other no matter how much I tried to relax and decide what to do next. So, I gave up and just watched the desert scenery unroll past the windows, while avoiding the urge to cry. I knew I was into something way over my head and felt helpless, not knowing what to do about it.

The bus arrived in Las Vegas after night had fallen, so I took a taxi to the youth hotel. When I checked in I told the receptionist there would be a man asking for Diane and would she please call me, no matter what the time. Then after sitting in my room for what seemed like ages I went out to get something to eat, again leaving instructions that anyone asking for me should wait. The bigger casinos have great restaurants with very cheap food. Once someone is hooked, casinos don't want to lose a player if they walk out to get food, so everything is laid on. Despite that, I rushed something down quickly and hurried back to the hotel where I irritated the receptionist by asking again if anyone had asked for me. She stopped chewing her gum.

"Look, honey, if anyone asks for you, you'll be the first to know—okay? Now let me do my work in peace." As I walked to the corridor she went back to flicking through her fashion magazine.

I went to bed and couldn't sleep so I turned on the light and read a book for an hour or two. I eventually fell into a troubled sleep and woke the next morning feeling tired and dispirited. William had not bothered to contact me and I had no idea what to do next. *Do I just continue with my trip to the Grand Canyon, should I contact the police as I had seen William attack those soldiers, or should I cut short my stop-over and go home now?*

After half an hour agonizing I gave up and went out to get some breakfast. As I passed the check-in counter there was a new woman on duty so I asked her if anyone had asked for Diane during the night but she shook her head. There was a man in a crumpled business suit, sitting in the only chair in the lobby.

"Good morning," he said from behind his newspaper as I passed, and I grumbled some kind of a reply.

I walked down the street, not wanting to go back to one of the casino's buffets but looking for a café where I might get a decent latte to kick start my morning. I found a little place that did not look too much like a slick franchise using good advertising to sell bad coffee, walked in and sat down. Before the waitress came to take my order the guy in the business suit sat down at the table too, not opposite me but beside me so he did not have his back to the door. I had been too wrapped up in my own thoughts to pay attention, but the surprise of having a stranger sit beside me without asking and the fear that he must have been following me woke me up fast. When I turned and looked, I could see it was William.

He smiled at me as I stared.

"Hi Diane, what's for breakfast?" His lightheartedness set off my anger again. *Why should he be so happy when my eyes were gritty from lack of sleep because he was turning my world upside down?*

"You look pleased with yourself," I snapped at him. "Enjoyed yourself yesterday, did you?"

I could almost see the walls come down around him as his face became impassive.

"Tell me what you want to know." But there was a gulf there between us again. *Oh damn, why do I have to be so combative when I feel off balance— and why does he have to be so bloody sensitive?*

We sat side by side uncomfortably, neither one looking in the other's direction. I finally said, "Look, I'm feeling pretty nervous right now—well actually terrified, and when I yell at you I don't always mean it. I think I would like you as a friend, but I still can't make up my mind if you are some crazy ax murderer or not. If the things you say are true I will help you if I can but I just don't know what to do. I'm sorry for being rude."

"Thanks for being straight with me. There is no way I can prove to you I am telling you the truth right now. You will simply have to decide for yourself. Before I came to meet you, I sent a message to the nearest Army base telling them where to find the two men who tried to arrest me yesterday. I figure that unless the Army uses a helicopter to find them I have about an hour and a half left till they have two eyewitness accounts of me being in this part of the country. Bear in mind they will also get a description of you, so you are going to have to decide very quickly if you want to be anywhere near me. Two people together are more obvious and easier to find than a single person."

He stopped as our breakfast appeared, and we ate in silence.

I finished first and said, "Couldn't you have left it a lot longer before alerting the Army about the men? You could be well away from here before they are found."

The thought that he was only here because I had asked him to explain himself and might be endangering his life because of me was not a comfortable one.

"No," he replied, "not safely. I hid the Jeep as best I could and the soldiers are well tied up, but once the day gets hot they could quickly die of dehydration or heat stroke and I won't let that happen. It was not their fault they tried to do their duty and they should not suffer for it if I can help it."

We each paid our bill and William looked through the telephone directory for Wells Fargo Bank branches. He asked the restaurant cashier which branch was nearest. I almost had to trot to keep up as William strode purposefully between the people on the pavement. However, when we reached the bank he slowed down and walked past.

"The last time I used my bank accounts was when I first escaped. I was almost caught then, so I know they are keeping track of any activity when transactions occur. Everything is recorded automatically, so they will know immediately I am withdrawing money, and even which branch I am at. I am hoping they have left my accounts open so I will use them again, and they can get a fix on my position. When the soldiers tell their story Army Intelligence will know I am in this part of the country anyway, so alerting them I am here by taking money out now does not make a lot of difference to my predicament."

We turned a corner down a side street. William, who was looking ahead, stopped and sent me back a little to a fashion dress shop.

"Wait by the window where you can see me walking back and join me."

I walked in but stepped back out in time to see him turn in to a hotel down the street. I went back in and waited by the mannequins in the storefront window. He came walking back along the street and I had to excuse myself from a determined shop assistant to get out of the store to meet him.

We sat for a few moments on a street bench.

"I have an old car parked in the street behind your hotel," William said. "If you want more answers you can meet me there after I leave the bank. I intend laying a false trail; I made a hotel reservation under an alias I have used before. If anyone remembers which way I leave from the bank they will send any pursuers away from your hotel and the car. It may take some time, so don't expect me too soon. But remember you can still walk away and continue your life as if you had never met me, which I think would be the smart thing to do. I will not wait long for you so if you decide to come, watch out for me."

William started walking back toward the bank without warning, so I had to hurry to catch up. As we got close he stopped and pointed out a smaller casino on the other side of the street. He suggested I go in and find somewhere to sit near a window so I could see the front of the bank.

"If I am right, agents of some kind will be at the bank within a few minutes of me withdrawing my money. It's likely they will already be on alert because of the missing soldiers. If you see agents or officers appear you will know it is unusual and that my story might be true."

I thought, *No I don't, maybe he will just rob the bank*, and said so to him. He looked crestfallen, stung again by my skepticism and suggested that I check him for any kind of weapon if I wanted, adding bitterly, "What am I going to do, threaten to bite them?"

As I walked over to the casino William headed resolutely toward the bank. The casino cashier cashed a traveler's check so I could get a handful of coins for the slot machines that were in lines near the front windows. As it was still early in the morning there was only one old man sitting on a stool mournfully putting coins into a machine and pulling the handle, so I was able to choose a machine where I could see the front of the bank. After a few pointless minutes of feeding the machine coins I felt as sad as the old man looked.

I decided that I had a good life with family waiting for me at home, so I should not screw it up getting involved with someone who could be dangerous or end up in prison for aiding a criminal. I was better off not meeting him at his car.

I saw William come out of the bank and went to stand by the window, looking at his back and silently saying my goodbyes with a heavy heart as he walked calmly away down the street. When he was only half way to the corner the security guard ran out the door of the bank and shouted something I could not hear through the glass. Without a glance backwards William bolted so the guard swung his pistol up, aimed and fired a shot in a single fluid movement. William stumbled sideways, falling against the plate-glass store front and pitched forward. Before he hit the ground, his body twisted and rolled. Even though he hit the ground hard, amazingly he came back up onto his feet and kept on running, but with a terrible limp. He was around the corner before the guard fired another shot. I think the guard realized he had been lucky not to hit a bystander with the first shot and was unwilling to risk it again.

- CHAPTER 3 -

ON THE RUN

I STOOD ROOTED TO THE SPOT in horror for what seemed like eternity before running to the entrance to the casino. I don't remember changing my mind, but I knew I had to follow William. By the time I reached the street I slowed to a walk to avoid drawing attention to myself. There was almost a crowd on the sidewalk now as people came out of the stores to see what had happened. I felt anonymous as I followed William's path down the street.

My heart went cold as I passed the window against which he had fallen and saw a faint smear of blood across it. By the time I got to the corner he was nowhere in sight, so I paused not knowing what to do next. I realized I had been hearing sirens for some time and that I needed to get away myself. I walked down the side street and called the first passing taxi to take me back to the hotel. I was getting too jittery walking out in the open on the sidewalk, hearing the sirens wailing and expecting the Spanish Inquisition to appear at any moment.

At the hotel, I gathered my things and repacked my backpack before going to reception and paying my bill—in cash. Shouldering the pack, I walked around to find the street behind the hotel was empty of people, but seemed filled with parked cars. I walked down one side and up the other, getting hot in the sun and thinking, *William's directions are not a lot of use to me; there are too many parked cars for me to guess which one might be his.*

As I could not think of anything better to do I sat in the shade under the fire escape ladder at the back of the building and read some of my book. By midday I was hot, thirsty and hungry, so I gave up waiting and trudged off, carrying my pack, to find a restaurant or supermarket or anything. I ate at a bar and stayed longer than I needed to, not really knowing what else to do. I was enjoying being out of the sun and thinking maybe air conditioning is not such a luxury after all.

While walking back I decided I would stay at the hotel for another night or two so William could find me if he was able to come looking—if he wanted to, anyway. I walked around for a last look at the street at the back of the building before checking in again. There was no one on the near side of the street I walked up so I crossed over and walked back along the other side. I found him propped up in a doorway, leaning against the door to keep the weight off his wounded leg.

He looked unconscious, but I rushed up and blurted, "William, are you all right?" It was a stupid question under the circumstances.

He started at the sound, then whispered, "Could I have some water, please?" He had not been able to drink since the early morning, had probably been in the sun for a while, along with having lost a lot of blood, so he was badly dehydrated. I gave him the bottle from my pack that I had refilled with iced water.

When he spoke again his voice was stronger, but I still needed to lean close to understand. "Despite what I said earlier I did wait because I hoped you would come . . . and I really need your help now."

It seemed as if it hurt him almost as much to have to depend on anyone for anything as the bullet wound was hurting.

"Can you drive for me? Because now that I've stopped moving I don't think I will be able to."

"Sure," I said, without telling him we drive on the other side of the road at home and I had never driven a left-hand drive before. It didn't seem the right time to mention it.

Moving slowly, he reached into a pocket and pulled out his car keys. He pointed out an old, dark blue Ford sedan and asked me to bring it down beside where he was sitting.

When I opened the trunk to put my pack in I saw William's old battered pack there already. As I pulled up beside William, he struggled to stand but was too weak, so he was forced to wait for my help. Even so, I was almost unable to get him up he was so heavy. He did not look that big because he was so well proportioned but as he leaned on me I realized he must be at least six feet tall.

Getting him into the car was another nightmare. Every movement of his leg caused him agony and he was fighting to keep from passing out again. I put the back of the seat down so he could lay on his good side and keep his wounded leg as straight as possible. I handed him the water bottle again and closed his door.

When I was sitting in the driver's seat I asked, "What do we do now?"

"We need to find another motel that is further away from the bank but still in Las Vegas. The roads leaving the city are likely to be watched for a few days, and we will be harder to find in the middle of the city with all the people around us than if we try to leave." The effort to speak left him gasping for breath and he seemed to collapse in on himself again, so I decided I would have to figure it out on my own.

I drove onto the main road but turned away from the city center toward the suburbs. When I drove past a gas station I parked in a secluded spot and walked back to get a city map. I found a list of motels in an accommodation guide and asked the guy working the full-service pumps if he could show me where the nearest ones were on the map.

I drove past the first two motels after stopping at each one and looking at the access. I did not fancy trying to haul William upstairs in full view of passers-by at the first or past the nosy receptionist at the second.

On my way to the next one I made a turn at a busy intersection and turned onto the left side of the street like I would at home. I swore loudly, shocked when I saw the oncoming cars, hit the brakes and jerked into a business entrance as the nearest car swerved around me blowing its horn. I sat shaking for a few moments before plucking up the courage to drive out again, this time on the right side of the road.

The third motel had a block of two room units at ground level. I was able to park the car in front of the door, making it possible to get William inside without too much difficulty. He was a little stronger, but fell exhausted onto the bed as soon as we were inside. I put the guest towels under him to try to keep the sheets on the bed from getting covered with blood. As he lay panting he asked me to find a pharmacy and get him some bandages, sterile wound dressings and some sports electrolyte drinks to help make up for the blood he had lost.

"You are going to die if you don't get a doctor soon. I'm not going to be responsible for that."

"Any doctor we called would report me as soon as he left the room because the wound is obviously from a bullet. You would be signing my death warrant because I am in no position to escape if they come for me now."

He then asked for a sharp knife, long-nosed pliers or splinter tweezers and some methylated spirits that I would need to get from a hardware store. As an afterthought he said, "Get a yard of three-eight cord as well. . . If I am asleep when you get back, you must wake me."

I told the receptionist my friend was sick and asked for directions to the nearest pharmacy. I got what he asked for along with a couple of rolls of paper towels and stopped at a 7-Eleven for some food.

When I got back William was in a fitful sleep, and I left him while I wrestled with my conscience over whether to disturb him when he was sleeping or whether to do as he asked. When I finally woke him, it was starting to get dark outside. He asked me to take his shoes off and then to help take his pants off. After struggling for a moment and causing William a lot of pain I decided it would be easier to cut them off, which was still not easy with the knife. I should have got scissors as well.

William was on his stomach and I was staring at the bullet hole in the back of his thigh when he said, "Either it must have been a small caliber gun or the bullet hit the bone because it is still in my leg. We need to get it out."

"What do you mean, WE?" I exclaimed.

He said calmly, "Yes, we, or rather you. I can't do it myself."

While I was washing all the tools with the methylated spirits William took the cord and tied a loop of it around the top of his leg. Then by putting the handle of a spoon through it and by twisting the cord tight, he made a passable tourniquet.

"You will have to take this off within twenty minutes or I could lose the leg. After you get the bullet out, put a few of the dressings on, then bind them with lots of bandages before taking the tourniquet off."

Between me rushing off to the bathroom and being sick and William passing out again from the pain, I managed to get the bullet out and his leg bandaged. William had been lucky that the bullet had not gone in too deeply or hit an artery.

About an hour later William woke up again. To my surprise he tried to struggle into a sitting position but almost passed out again from the pain as he put pressure on his leg. It seemed ridiculous to me that he was even trying, and I said so.

"When I meditate I always sit in the *seiza* position on my knees like you see in Japanese martial arts. Just sitting like that helps me calm and center my mind and I must do that tonight. If I stay lying down I will keep falling asleep."

When I asked why he was being such an idiot he said, "Because I am getting weaker and may not have the strength or endurance by tomorrow to do what I have to. That would be disastrous for us both."

He had to settle for a semi-reclining position, propped up with pillows and cushions from the couch. He closed his eyes and his breathing slowed so I left the bedroom and closed the door.

After flicking between TV channels for probably two hours, the news came on. I was brooding and barely paying attention until the TV anchor said there had been an armed robbery at a bank in the city today. After showing some footage of the front of the bank there was an interview with an eyewitness who said how terrifying it had been and how the customers at the bank had been saved by the brave security guard who fought the robber and wounded him during his getaway. This was followed by a grainy bank security camera picture of William, who the anchor identified as William Durante, a US Army deserter. This was followed by pictures of a younger William in uniform. The newscaster said William had killed two men when he broke out of a military prison about eighteen months ago, and provided a few minor details about him like his height and hair and eye color. A police official then appeared on the screen, appealing for the public to come forward with any information that might help capture the fugitive, finishing by saying he was known to be "armed and dangerous."

I spent a terrible night on the couch without much sleep, thinking William must be a dangerous criminal after all. That made me a criminal, too, as I was helping him evade arrest. The last thing I wanted was to be spending the next few years of my life in a US prison.

By the time morning came I had decided if he was dangerous I would have to turn him in before more people got hurt. I sat in anguish by the phone trying to pluck up the courage to dial 911, but feeling grief stricken at the thought of betraying him. But, in the end, I couldn't do it until I knew for sure. So, I decided to see if I could get some answers I could be sure of before doing anything else.

When I looked into the room early in the morning William was finally sleeping deeply so I let him be. He began stirring about mid-morning, so I walked in and without any preamble confronted him with the story I had seen on the news. William looked a little stunned at my outburst as I accused him of being a deserter, killer and bank robber. He said nothing but swung off the bed, and my heart missed several beats. I was alone with an accused killer. While he struggled painfully over to take something out of his pack I was imagining him looking for guns or knives and me winding up as his latest victim. As he rummaged I was trying to make up my mind to attack him or to make a run for it. I surreptitiously lifted a heavy glass vase from the table beside the door.

William noticed his tattered trousers by the bed and sitting back down to pick them up, pulled out a large envelope that had been stuffed into one of the pockets. As he shuffled through it I could see it was filled mostly with hundreds and some thousand-dollar bills. He pulled a printed receipt from the bank from the envelope showing the amount of his withdrawal with his name on the account.

"They don't usually give bank robbers receipts, do they? . . . I have to go to the bathroom," he said blandly, and moved off the bed and staggered awkwardly with occasional grunts of pain out the bedroom door, toward the toilet.

I tried to put down the vase without him noticing and helped him limp across the lounge. Then I remembered the terrible state his leg was in by the time I got the bullet out last night. The thoughts that were going through my head suddenly came out in a torrent.

"How can you walk like that? With all that happened yesterday you should be dead. There is a lot more to this than meets the eye, isn't there?"

He replied with a nod as he closed the door behind him.

– CHAPTER 4 –

A DECISION OF SORTS

WHEN WILLIAM RETURNED to the dining room he continued ignoring my questions.

"I would like to check how the bullet wound is healing," he said, "then we can talk after we have had something to eat."

I helped him remove the bandage, but while plenty of blood soaked through it, I was stunned to see the hole in his leg had gone a long way toward healing.

William grinned, saying, "It looks good and is obviously not infected. I'll be as good as new within a week."

After I had dressed and re-bandaged his leg we ate what was left of last night's dinner with mugs of scalding coffee.

When I was cleaning up William said, "Oh well, I suppose it is time we introduced ourselves. All I know about you is your name is Diane and you have an accent that makes it pretty clear you are not from the United States."

So I told him a bit about myself.

"I come from New Zealand and have been in England for a couple of years working as a computer programmer and touring whenever I had enough money. At home, we call it 'The Big O.E.,' meaning traveling overseas when we leave school or university to see more of the world. I am only in the US for a month for a holiday on my way home. Now tell me about you and what's going on here. That's what's really important to me at the moment. I need to know what I am caught up in—and why."

He thought for a while then said, "I can't answer the why for myself either, but for the last eighteen months I have always lived by a strict rule never to involve anyone in my problems—and this is the first time I have ignored it. I can't help feeling breaking that rule has gotten me in this predicament now."

Seeing the dark look on my face as I considered this, he continued quickly. "Sorry, I'm not blaming you or anything. I've been on the run for a long time now with the military as well as other government agencies constantly dogging my every step, but they have only got this close to catching or killing me once before. I had no intention to involve you either, but I was just making decisions that felt right, if you know what I mean," and went quiet.

Okay—so he hadn't fallen head over heels at the first sight of me. When I looked at him with a raised eyebrow he tried to explain.

"Most of the time the decisions we make are meaningless and are of no real consequence, like what am I going to have for breakfast or even should I quit my job or leave my lover. People find replacements and though their circumstances may change they don't usually change who they are in any real way. So really for them the effects of these decisions are trivial.

"When I sat down beside you on that bus in LA it was an impulse," he continued. "I was feeling tired and harried and it just seemed like something amusing that I thought was meaningless at the time. But when you walked up to me at the truck stop and we yelled at each other, I knew that somehow I had to take some time and explain what I could to you, even though it was against my better judgment. That was why I followed you back to the diner. I have remained free this long by doing nothing that attracts notice. I stay anonymous, and therefore invisible, to most people. But as I said, it felt right. I could have chosen differently and just walked away, but I know I would have lost something if I had. Call it a gut feeling if you like, but it's more than that."

He paused to refill his coffee then continued.

"As for me, well, leaving out the unimportant bits, I am William Durante and I am originally from North Carolina. After leaving school I joined the Army as a way to get away from home. I couldn't afford college, so I saw the Army as a way to get more education and thought maybe it would turn into a good career. I couldn't have been more wrong there. Anyway, while I was in combat something weird happened to me that no one, least of all me at the time, could explain. However, my problems really began after my superiors sent reports back to the US and it ended up with me being flown home under guard, locked up 'for my own protection,' and used like a guinea pig. I eventually escaped, or deserted, depending on how you look at it, but I did not kill anyone."

The effort of being up and talking was already taking its toll on him though he was too proud to admit it. I could see his hand shaking as he lifted his coffee and told him to go back to bed and sleep some more. He agreed reluctantly, and I helped him back into the bedroom.

I watched TV for a while but when lunchtime came around William was deeply asleep so I quietly locked the door and walked to the mall where I had found the 7-Eleven last evening. I listlessly ate some forgettable takeaway then went to a movie theatre as I couldn't think what else to do. I still had not really made up my mind to trust William and didn't want to rush back.

After the movie, still undecided, I bought enough food for the two of us for dinner and reluctantly made my way back to the motel.

The reception I received from William was not what I was expecting. He was lying on his good side on the couch so he could watch the door. He jumped up when it opened, then collapsed back painfully when he saw it was me.

"Where have you been?" he demanded.

I was caught off guard by his anger so I snapped back, "Out walking and getting you some food. I did not know I had to apply for your permission, and thank you for your appreciation of my efforts."

I had closed the door but stayed standing beside it, glaring at him while he glared back. I was determined not to back down or to move away from the door until I had a better idea of what was going on in his head. After an icy silence with the two of us staring at each other he said coldly, "Doesn't it occur to you they might be looking for you?"

"They are looking for you, not me," I countered. "It's your problem, not mine."

"No, it's not," he almost yelled, his anger or frustration flaring again. "Use your head. They will have a good description of you from the two Ranger soldiers who tried to grab you. They know you were sitting with me and the fact you ran off after they tried to question you means they will not believe that you are innocent."

"But they didn't question me; they tried to abduct me," I argued.

"That's not how they will see it. I proved to you this morning I did not rob that bank but that the government is quite happy to lie about it. Whatever they told that security guard convinced him to try to kill me with that shot rather than let me go. Human life means nothing to them. They are quite happy to kill to preserve their secrets. It is the same for you now too. They will kill you before letting you go, so think again if you believe it is not your problem. This is your life on the line now too and they simply don't care."

All the fight drained out of me leaving me feeling cold and queasy as the enormity of the situation struck home. If I were an ordinary criminal, the government would play by the rules and I would be handled according to the law, but this was different. There were no rules here, only survival—or not.

After a pause William continued in the background, though I was lost in my thoughts.

"I have no idea how thorough they are likely to be. They may even check recent car sales as they know within an hour or two when I arrived here, so they may have the license number for my car. I doubt it though as I have not bought a car before, so it is out of character for me. If the soldiers were observant, they will have noticed your funny accent and figured out you are a foreigner so they might be cross checking with immigration. If so, they will recognize your photo if they can pull one up from the database. There are far too many possibilities for us to consider them all."

William had stopped and was now looking at me in a way that felt kind rather than hostile. I was still standing by the door but unwilling or unable to comment; I don't really know which. I finally walked over and dropped the bags of food onto the table, then slumped onto one of the two worn chairs. I don't like to look weak and though I tried hard to stop them, tears were starting to run down my cheeks. I gave in and wiped them off with a sniff.

William watched me for a while, then said gently, "I'm sorry." I looked up and could see the strain on his face. He had been genuinely worried or afraid for me, and I realized his reaction when I returned was more an explosion of relief than anger. No doubt he was expecting the Secret Service to be knocking on the door rather than me, but I was too upset to break the silence. He left me to my thoughts and though he resisted he gradually fell asleep.

He woke a little later, stiff and hurting from sleeping cramped on the couch. I made us both some dinner and then sent him off to the bedroom for the night. I repeated my late-night TV vigil to keep my mind distracted and from running round in ever diminishing circles. I watched the news often, but there was no further mention of William's supposed robbery or requests for the public to look out for him.

In the morning, William dressed and rebandaged his leg without my help. At William's insistence, we stayed in our room all day, even though I argued there had been no mention of me at all on the news, so no one would be looking for me. He said government agents would be secretly looking for me and we shouldn't take chances.

It's always worst when you know you are in a dire situation, when you seem helpless and there is nothing you can do to take your mind off it. William again spent most of the day sleeping, so I was left alone. After a late dinner, he asked what I wanted to do next as he thought he could probably get by on his own in a day or two.

If I was to get away from him for the rest of my time in the US and catch my flight home that should be the end of it. There was nothing concrete to connect the two of us. But having wrestled with possibilities all day I knew if I backed out now I would never forgive myself and told him so, adding with a smile, "You won't get rid of me that easily."

He smiled back as he replied, "I was kind of hoping you would say that."

But then he sighed, "So what do we do now? I'm all out of ideas."

Next morning, the third since William had been shot, he was able to walk almost normally. His healing was still proceeding at a phenomenal rate.

After tossing ideas around with William and getting nowhere I finally said, "I came here to see some of this country. Normally I would stay at youth hostels or with backpackers, but as you have a car, couldn't we buy tents and camp in a national park or something like that?"

William turned the idea over in his mind for a while.

"Okay, I have always preferred big cities. So many people around makes you invisible, but I guess they have always found me anyway, no matter how I have tried to hide; so it probably won't make any difference."

"That doesn't make sense, how can they *always* find you in a country this size?"

He looked bitter, saying, "It's a long story, and it's going to make me sound crazier than you already think I am. So, if you don't mind, we'll talk about it later."

Feeling annoyed, I said, "What if I do mind? You'll have to trust me sometime."

Later that afternoon, though William obviously disapproved of my going out, I went on a spending spree with some of his money. When I asked him how come he had so much he had said he did not spend much money while he was on active service overseas so a lot of pay had accumulated in his bank account. After my first attempt at driving in a left-hand drive car I was not feeling confident enough to try again so I got a taxi to a camping store. I paid them a little extra to have two small tents and other cooking and camping equipment delivered to our motel and then went to a 7-Eleven to get enough food for a week or so.

I got a taxi back late in the afternoon. My despair evaporated as I enjoyed the desert heat, such a contrast to the English winter I was in less than a week before. However, my good humor turned instantly to panic as I looked through the motel suite and found it empty.

I decided to go and look for William rather than stay and let my fears multiply. I looked around the motel complex first, then strode purposefully down the road toward the mall. I've learned from watching managers in the companies where I've worked that if you remain forceful, active and look like you know what you are doing, no one questions you.

There was no sign of him, and I quickly decided I was wasting my time. So I walked back toward the motel, but more slowly now as I was paying more attention to my surroundings.

As I walked in the entrance I saw an older man who was sitting on the wooden bench in the shade of the only tree at the front of the motel. He winked at me, which caused me to take another look. *William?* His hair and beard had been neatly trimmed and both were a light reddish shade, though this was hard to see under the hat that also hid some of his features. He wore geeky glasses and held a small faded briefcase on his lap which, together with the desultory way he sat, had made him seem middle aged. *He obviously has a penchant for disguises*, I thought.

"I got you again," he smiled. Bad move. I was already feeling really annoyed with him.

"You bastard, I was terrified you were caught, killed or god only knows what and wondering if I needed to escape or hide, and you're playing games."

William was still looking pleased with himself.

"This is deadly serious. I'm here, far enough away not to be noticed, so I can see what's going on around the motel. Equally, I want to look different enough when we leave here for observers to casually glance over me, to see there is someone in the car, but know that that's not who they are looking for. Let's go inside, there are some new developments we need to talk about."

CHAPTER 5

HIS STORY STARTS

WILLIAM STARTED TALKING as soon as I had closed the door.

"I'm almost sure they know we are in this area and will be narrowing down the possibilities over the next day or so, so we need to go. I'm hoping tomorrow won't be too late."

To me this just sounded like more paranoia.

"Bullshit, they couldn't possibly know where we are."

"I just know, all right," he was adamant. "I went outside to watch the cars driving past. At least one had agents."

"Yeah right," I said, so he talked on, trying to justify how he was so certain his hunters were close.

William gave up. "Will you just humor me and go and pay our bill now so we can leave first thing in the morning?"

"Only if you will tell me everything so I can decide for myself if any of this makes sense."

He agreed he would, but I still made him give his word before I paid the bill. When I got back he was working distractedly with the food on the bench without achieving anything, so I told him to sit down and rest while I made dinner. We ate quietly with a minimum of small talk as I was still angry at what I saw as his flippant treatment of me. He was trying to be good by not annoying me any further.

After dinner, he asked me to turn the TV on.

"No, not until you tell me more about what's going on ... you promised."
I could see he didn't like being told what to do.

We waited silently for some time as he got himself comfortable and
decided what he should say.

"The event that caused all this happened while I was on a tour of active
duty in Iraq. My platoon had been sent as part of the battle plan to free
a northern town that had been occupied by insurgents. It was something
we had done before in other towns and we had been picked to go in first
because we were Rangers and we were good at it.

"You have no idea what it's like in the middle of a fire fight. The
enormous fear but also the adrenaline rush that makes you feel incredibly
alive. At close range, our field artillery and tanks were pounding the
military targets while rockets and mortars were being fired back at us. We
couldn't call in an air strike because the town was still full of civilians who
had refused to leave. My company had moved into position and we were
waiting at the front line, such as it was, to be sent in. We were still in our
armored personnel carriers, but the noise was terrible. Our job was to enter
the town and to try to distinguish between the civilian population and the
insurgents as soon as the barrage stopped.

"This sort of battle is far worse than open warfare because there
is no way to tell the difference between a civilian and an enemy until
someone picks up a gun, and by then it can be too late for you. You don't
know where the guns are hidden and soldiers may have walked past a
boy half a dozen times before he pulls out an AK47 and just blazes
away, or it may be bombs, mines or traps like tripwires left behind that
get you. No matter how good you are it is still Lady Luck who decides
if you live or die.

"Each soldier learns to deal with the fear in his own way. I had been
through many battles and knew that all I could do was wait, for minutes
or hours—we had no idea how long. This may sound insane, but in the
middle of all that mayhem I was meditating to calm my mind and try to
shut out the fear.

"I had done it many times but something, I don't know what, was different this time. When we got the order to go I was in a kind of trance. I followed the others without thinking about it because it was what I always did. My friends were running from cover to cover, firing back whenever they paused and even as they ran. The odd thing was I felt no fear. I knew I was completely safe and absentmindedly put my gun on the ground, not even sure why I was holding it. I ambled along behind the rest of the soldiers but made no effort to hide because I knew I didn't need to. I know I was hit by bullets, but they left no marks and I could sometimes hear them ricocheting off.

"Our soldiers became pinned down by heavy resistance, but I walked off further into the town leaving them behind. I remember my commander, Major Laurence, was yelling at me as I left, calling me every swearword under the sun, trying to get me to take cover but it just didn't seem important.

"The opposing fighters melted away in front of me as they realized something they couldn't explain was happening, and their superstition got the better of them. I was soon left alone though I could still hear the fighting in other parts of the city.

"By the time the fighting was over I had rejoined our soldiers, but was still in that altered state of mind. Major Laurence had me locked up, *for my own protection*, and immediately sent a highest priority report to HQ. These can sometimes take days to get a reply, but in this case firm orders arrived within a couple of hours that I was to be held in the most secure facility available and no one apart from him was to speak to me under any circumstances. Any soldiers who had witnessed the incident were to be confined to barracks and were not to discuss the incident at all. An investigation team was being flown over to take charge and nothing was to be done until they arrived.

"The first thing the team of specialists did when they arrived was to interrogate me using all the usual stand-over techniques the Army does so well. None of this had any effect on me. So they tried to inject me with sodium pentothal but the needles just bent on my skin. They tried beating me, but that made no difference either. By now they were starting to get scared, so they put me in every type of restraint they could think of and flew me back to the States.

"I heard through the grapevine later that they hung around at the base for another week and even went out to the town and looked around where we had been fighting. They convinced the rest of my friends that they hadn't seen anything out of the ordinary and that I had simply gone nuts from the fear. It was easy enough to believe. Nobody in their right mind puts their gun down and walks casually through a pitched battle. Everybody was told that I was being shipped stateside for treatment."

I could hear the bitterness in William's voice.

"All my former friends didn't think twice when high command said I had deserted later. They knew I was crazy anyway."

William got up and went to make some coffee. Although he was healing at a remarkable rate, he was still moving gingerly, and I was irritated again by his refusal to ask for help.

"Why didn't you ask me to do that?"

"Because I didn't need to."

"You don't have to suffer for the sake of it."

He just shrugged. *Damn his stupid machismo. Can't he see we're in this mess together? It wouldn't hurt to let his defenses down or even, God forbid, accept some kindness without assuming there must be a catch.*

After handing me a cup of coffee and sitting down with his own, William continued.

"Although I have lost most of what I could do when I was in that strange state of mind, my mind is still a lot more sensitive now than it was before the incident happened. I know things without knowing why. I sometimes can sense what other people are thinking and I know when I am in danger even when there is no outward sign. That is why I am sure they are closing in on us now. I can feel it or sense them or something; I don't know how to explain it, but I know trusting this ability has saved my life more than once in the past eighteen months, so I'll trust it now."

I was trying to digest all the information.

"That is an awful lot to take in. Can you prove any of it?"

I didn't mean to imply I didn't believe him, but he seemed to take it that way.

He snapped, "Obviously not or I wouldn't just be telling you, would I?"

We lapsed into an uncomfortable silence again while I brooded over his touchiness, his tacit assumption that I had no right to question him, or worse, that he was above questioning.

We sat for a while, staring at the TV that I had turned on as a distraction. As I was still feeling uncomfortable I was surreptitiously watching William so I noticed he was becoming agitated. After about fifteen minutes of not being able to sit still he suddenly blurted out, "Get our gear in the car as quickly as possible."

As I got up I replied, "A please would be nice."

I could see him bridle at what he felt was me being difficult, but he kept his temper in check and with a sigh said, "Please, it is vital we go now."

I went and got his pack from the bedroom and brought the rest of his gear for him to put in.

He said, "Get your own pack ready and make sure you leave nothing behind."

I put in my toilet bag from the bathroom and some other odds and ends, but as I put the pack over my shoulder and went to go out the door he looked up and said, "Sorry, I've changed my mind, just leave it by the door."

I dropped it where he had said and walked around the couch to face him. Icy shock ran through me when I saw that he was screwing a silencer onto a long-barreled handgun. He saw the look on my face.

"What do you expect me to do? There is a whole army of people out there trying very hard to kill me and they all carry guns. Do you really expect me to be all honorable and noble and walk around defenseless? That is a good way to commit suicide; I'm a soldier after all. Whether you believe it or not I have no intention of killing anyone, but I find a gun in your hand is a bargaining point that is hard to argue with . . . and it would be best if you don't come with me now. I don't want them seeing you with me."

"You keep insisting there are enemies outside our door, but I haven't seen them."

He waved his hand to forestall my arguments without seeming to realize there was a gun in it.

"Don't bother trying to change my mind, you are simply not coming. As soon as you are sure there is no one watching, go to the casino at the end of the street and stay the night there. If I am able to, I will come in the morning while people are coming to work and there are lots of cars. I'll meet you on the ground floor somewhere."

I was staring at him silently.

"I have always kept my word to you, I will come back—if I can."

He finished with his pack and stood, struggling, balancing precariously on his good leg, so I helped him get it on his shoulders. As he walked to the door he said, "Keep out of sight. You can watch through the curtains but don't give away you are here. Nothing may happen, anyway . . . God willing, I'll see you in the morning," and turned out the lights before stepping out.

I went to the window and shifted the curtain as little as I could and still see past. I watched him throw his pack in the back, get in and drive slowly out onto the road, turning right, away from the casino, toward the darker end of the street. As he drove off, a car door opened on the other side of the street and a man stepped out onto the road, blocking William's escape, pointing a gun straight at William through the windshield.

William stopped rather than trying to drive over him, which I felt strangely grateful for. The man walked slowly around to the driver's door and he seemed to say something as he reached to pull the door open. I couldn't see whether his aim on William wavered as he opened the door or whether he saw William's gun was trained on him, but after a moment's stalemate, both his hands went up in the air and he took a step back, throwing the gun away as he did. I guess the man decided William had a whole lot less to lose than he did. I saw a dim muzzle flash and thought, *NO! William's shot him*. To my relief the bonnet of the car dropped and I realized William had shot the front tire of the man's car. William's lights went out and he gunned his car toward the end of the street, turning left with a squeal of tires. The man bent down, scrambling in the dark to pick up his gun off the road and fired a couple of times as William disappeared around the corner. He leapt in his car and after a moment tried to chase William but with the flat front tire wasn't able to take the corner and crashed into the curb on the other side of the road. A moment later a second car raced down the street. It screeched to a halt by the crashed car. The driver jumped in and it roared off, but William was long gone.

Okay, so I was wrong about the agents. I guess I'll have to apologize later— if there is a later.

– CHAPTER 6 –

INTO THE FURNACE

I DIDN'T HESITATE. As soon as the second car was gone I threw my pack on and walked out the door, closing it quietly behind me. I walked out to the road in the shadows, avoiding the brightly lit pools on the pavement under the motel lights. I was trying hard to be inconspicuous while at the same time trying to be nonchalant and not look furtive. I was terrified.

I started to calm down after I had taken a few paces down the sidewalk and no mysterious figures had appeared to drag me off to an unknown fate. By the time I reached the casino at the end of the street my heart had stopped racing and my breathing was almost back to normal, so I was able to go straight to the desk and ask if they had a room for the night. They did and no one batted an eyelid at me turning up late, alone and without a car.

The room was surprisingly reasonable. After sitting for half an hour to regain my nerve, I changed into something a little more fitting for an evening at a casino—well the best I could do under the circumstances. No one I know carries an evening dress and high heels in her backpack.

I just went out to walk around the casino to explore. I'm not one of those people who can sit down and accept fate without fighting. I needed to do something to burn off the nervous energy.

After buying some casino chips I spent an entertaining hour or two walking between the gaming tables or sitting for a while and placing small bets or playing hands of blackjack. When I got bored with that I looked around the building. On the third floor, I found an excellent all-you-can-eat buffet restaurant—and that's what I did.

Feeling replete and tired I went back to my room and, considering the circumstances, slept surprisingly well.

I had set the alarm to wake me early as William had not given a time and I was determined not to miss him. I forced myself to shower and get moving, regretting some of the complimentary drinks from the night before. I had a meager breakfast and went down to the ground floor. The glitter and excitement had faded with the night. The cleaning crews were still visible and the few patrons at the poker machines were not early risers but those who could not face giving up on their losses and going to bed.

It was more than an hour before William arrived. It doesn't sound like much but when your life suddenly becomes out of control with fear around every corner, an hour is an eternity.

I saw him sauntering casually between the tables. I waved to catch his eye when he glanced in my direction and I saw he had shaved off his beard and somehow removed the red rinse from his hair.

As he wandered up I greeted him tersely with, "You certainly took your time."

"It's not even eight o'clock yet," he said defensively.

"Sorry, I'm a bit on edge."

We went to my room and got my pack, returned the key, and went to his car. I voiced my amazement at the size of the car park, made more obvious as it was largely empty, to William. There was even an area with some RVs and Winnebagos.

"During the holidays, this place will be full," William said.

As we walked to the car he said once he realized he was not being followed and as he had reacted without any plan, he decided to follow the advice he had given me. He had spent the night at another casino some distance away.

Once we were in the car and William was driving I asked, "Where are we going?"

"East, that's where the Grand Canyon is, anyway. We can decide where exactly we want to go later."

"Shouldn't we change the car or go back to using buses? Won't the agents be looking for the car?"

"It was dark and I turned the lights off as I drove away from the first man so the license plate light couldn't light the plate and give the number away. Without a license number, it would be nearly impossible to find a particular one of such a common car as we have. Besides, they don't usually conduct major searches when looking for me as that brings their activities to the public eye. They would rather their interest in me wasn't advertised."

William was feeling buoyant. I commented acerbically on his good humor as I was feeling overwhelmed by the narrowness of our escape.

"Surviving for another day has that effect on me," he said dryly. The road signs marked Hoover Dam's approach, and I asked William to stop so I could do the tourist thing. Once I saw the dam and Lake Mead stretched out behind it I even dug my old Canon camera out of my backpack and took some pictures. Coming from New Zealand, where the countryside is always green, it seemed incongruous to be driving through a desert, only to come across a vast hydroelectric power station, and then go back to driving through the desert again.

Later, after watching cars and scenery go past and quietly mulling over the last night as I did, I said, "You said before they always find you. Those men in the cars last night were checking out the street we were in. They can't have been doing that across the entire city. How did they know where we were or at least the general area?"

William sighed. "Because someone told them." He fell silent and needed some threats of a tantrum before he would explain.

He was wrestling with memories he found distasteful and painful. "When they brought me home they took me to Fort Bragg army base. It's close enough to Washington for its masters to visit and keep a regular eye on me, but remote enough, in North Carolina, to be largely ignored. Mostly Fort Bragg is a regular military base, but it also acts as a front for a clandestine unit that is researching the use of psychic abilities, mental powers like telepathy, for use in warfare. Very few in the Pentagon know it exists and I'll bet the president doesn't know either. They call the unit and its area of research The Prometheus Project or just Prometheus.

"Of course, being the military, they don't trust their guinea pigs, the men or the two women that I saw, they are holding there who have shown special talents, any more than they do anyone else. They preferred to keep their most important guinea pigs apart, obeying the primary military rule of divide and conquer, but occasionally we were allowed to work together if it seemed to be for the good of the many projects that they were working on. They had to allow us some kind of social interaction, too, to keep us sane, and were not willing to let us mix with regular soldiers at the base or our guards so by default, later on, I got to mix with some of the less dangerous or valuable prisoners. However, long term solitary confinement was one of the many methods used to break the wills of recalcitrant experimentees, and I know there were some I never met.

"Because of the typical paranoia of the military mind, the top brass used a couple of mind readers or telepaths who kept an eye on the rest of the inmates and reported back on their undying loyalty—or lack of it no doubt. The telepaths were quartered separately and not allowed to ever mix with the rest of us. Partly this was to prevent any familiarity or friendship developing between them and us, and also because the rest of us detested their intrusions into our privacy. It was like a game of chess among some of the prisoners there to devise ways of circumventing the mental surveillance.

"Some were quite good at it and most were able to conceal anything they chose to from the younger one of them. He was not much more than a boy, found during his first tour of duty, and either his talent or his self-confidence and determination were not that strong. I never met him in the short time I was there, but the impression I got from the others was that in some way his will had been broken. When he was first brought to Fort Bragg he had been forced to submit to his much stronger colleague and the resulting inferiority and resentment he felt made it unlikely he would ever develop his ability very far. It was relatively easy to hide your deeper thoughts from him or mislead him. Belief in yourself is vital. Sometimes you will lose but don't ever submit or give up.

"The other one was different. One of my fellow prisoners called him

Argus as a joke, and the name stuck. We all called him Argus after that. He could really see into your mind and could smash down most people's defenses if they tried to fight his intrusions. While I was physically invulnerable he was not able to touch my mind either, but after I lost the ability he was set on me as part of the attempt to achieve control of my talent. I still have nightmares about those interrogations.

"I know they are using him and his abilities to track me and help locate me. If he was with the agents last night I have no doubt he could have pinpointed the motel we were in, but he is far too valuable for Prometheus to risk losing him. They won't take him out of their secure facility, at least not for someone as unimportant as me. They are right about the need to keep him safe too. When I said I would not kill anyone with that gun, I was not thinking about him. If he was in front of me I would not hesitate."

"Do you hate him that much?" I asked.

"I did once," William shrugged, "but not now. As time has passed I understand him a lot better. Argus is a prisoner in his own way, both of his talent and of his keepers. Behind their veneer of civilized urbanity, they are vile, sadistic men who are as afraid of him as they are afraid of anything not in complete subjugation to their wills. They will never release him. When he tried to look into my mind the link worked both ways; I could also see some of his mind. He was once a kind and gentle man, but they have bent him completely to their whims. He has no hope of a decent life and it would be a kindness to release him from his torment."

William lapsed into silence but after some time murmured, "Now that I think about it, what I really hate most, I guess what I am really afraid of, is that he is what I would become if I had not escaped—or if I am recaptured. That horrifies me. If I had the chance, I would free him the only way I can, and I pray he would do the same for me if situations were reversed."

We drove in silence for a long time.

We reached Grand Canyon Village sometime late morning. We put some food and water in our day packs and walked to the head of the trail that leads into the canyon. Bright Angel Trail starts from the South Rim at nearly seven thousand feet high and so the air was still relatively cool when we started down.

As we walked down the trail we were passed by groups of mules carrying tourists. The idea of riding a swaying mule down that path with the huge drop on one side held no appeal to me at all.

We descended nearly three thousand feet to Indian Gardens before walking out almost a mile to look down onto the Colorado River, over a thousand feet lower still. The heat had increased as we descended into the canyon and with the sun rising higher it felt to me like we were walking in a furnace. We decided not to continue down to the river as we were already overheated and exhausted.

It was late evening, getting dark by the time we made it back to the South Rim. It had been a mistake to start out so late in the day. The climb back up in the afternoon heat had turned into a grim ordeal. Even William's usual mask of stoicism slipped and was not able to conceal his suffering.

"So your leg does hurt," I said.

"Maybe . . . a little. I'm more tired than sore."

Frankness. Finally! I thought.

After resting in the car for a time we drove to the nearest campground and William found the strength from somewhere to help pitch our tents.

Despite my exhaustion, sleep didn't come easily. The incredible experience and the grandeur of the scenery had not been able to keep my mind from churning over William's unlikely revelations of his involvement in secret military programs, the idea of mind powers and my skepticism.

However, as I lay in my sleeping bag I realized William walking down into the canyon and then back again should be impossible. I had taken it for granted. Given the severity of his bullet wound he should be lying in a hospital bed. The pieces fitted together with a clunk and I slipped into a dreamless sleep. I finally came to terms with my situation and started to trust William.

CHAPTER 7

A HOLIDAY OF SORTS

I WOKE THE NEXT MORNING feeling hung over from dehydration and fatigue but light, as if a great weight had been taken off my shoulders. The Grand Canyon was like a watershed for me. Despite the fact that we were being pursued by all the legions of darkness I was feeling at peace with my decision to trust William completely. There was a rightness to the choice that overwhelmed my reticence and that I have never once regretted since.

That sense of peace is unusual for me and I was so silent while we packed our tents, drove to a café and ate breakfast that William became unnerved.

"So what have I done to upset you this time?"

I smiled sweetly and replied, "Nothing at all."

My mood changed once we were in the car and moving again.

"We're headed for Canyon de Chelly," he said.

"Thanks for asking," I pouted. Actually, I was okay with his choice. "Won't Argus just pinpoint us again as soon as we stop, and how come they never caught you long ago if he is that good?"

"As to the first part of your question, I think it is harder for him to use his talent as distances get farther away, and particularly in places where he has never been. That is part of the reason I have spent most of my time on the West Coast. It is a long way from him. It will have taken him a great deal of effort and concentration to locate me so precisely over such a long distance, and I know that will have taken a considerable toll on him. We should be safe for some time.

"As to the second, I feel that Argus has let me escape several times. He has served his masters and done as he is ordered, but I feel certain he has not always done all he could to ensure my capture. Our battles have left a grudging respect between the two of us and a glimmer of understanding. We recognize each other as kindred spirits, even if we are on opposing sides. He does not hate me and I no longer hate him, and I know we both wish we could be free."

We arrived at Canyon de Chelly to find access to the canyon is mostly limited and we would have to book and wait for a tour of the canyon floor which we didn't want to do. We drove up the canyon rim to the one trail open to visitors, the White House Ruin trail and walked into the canyon, which is part of the Navajo reservation and holds ruined buildings from the Pueblo Peoples, also called the Anasazi. The ruins were worth the effort to see. There were the remains of rock buildings, perched in a large cave in a sheer wall of the canyon and on the floor of the canyon just below.

I did not sleep well and heard William stirring outside the tent early next morning. I shifted in my sleeping bag so I could watch him through the front of my tent. He was facing out over the valley, looking away from our tents and doing some kind of gently flowing movements or routines with lots of breaks between segments. He continued to practice for nearly an hour. Though the morning was still chilly there were beads of sweat visible on his forehead when he finished and walked back toward the campsite. He was not aware I was watching him; his smile was radiant.

He finished his routine and as he turned to go back to his tent, saw me staring at him from the warmth of my sleeping bag.

"Time to get up. Let's make the most of the day."

"I plan to," I said. "By staying here and reading for at least another hour."

He wandered off and poured himself a mug of water before putting some trainers on to go running. I was still watching him, and he was about to go when he looked at the mug that still was almost half full. He picked it up and walked over to my tent.

"Okay," he said with a grin on his face, "time to get up or I throw the water in."

"You wouldn't dare," I threatened. It was definitely the wrong thing to say. He threw it in without a second thought. I jumped out in my jammies and tried to thump him. He fended me off for a few moments, both of us laughing, then took my arm in a flowing movement that easily caused me to lose my balance and took me to the ground.

"Give in?" he asked.

"Do I have any choice?"

He let go, feeling happy with himself.

"I'm going for a run," he said. "I'll see you later."

He came back to the campground about half an hour later. While he was away I had dressed and organized some breakfast for us, most importantly my coffee. As we were sitting at a camp table eating and talking, I was still a little annoyed and teased him.

"What were you doing earlier? Is that the best they can teach the Rangers these days?"

"No," he replied soberly, "but there has been enough anger and violence in my life. I choose a different way to live now. I was performing some exercises I learned from a t'ai chi teacher a few years ago, just before I joined the Army. I will show you if you like."

This became part of our routine for the next few days. Every morning we would practice t'ai chi or mostly chi gong, eat breakfast, then go hiking for the rest of the day. We never talked much while we walked, content to enjoy the scenery and each other's company.

– CHAPTER 8 –

WHO NEEDS TRAINING?

WILLIAM WAS A HARD TASKMASTER. My mind was obviously wandering during one of our morning workouts so William stopped.

"A common feature of the soft or internal martial arts is training yourself to focus fully in the present. Giving all your attention to what you are doing right now with no idle thoughts of the future or past. Not living for your hopes or wallowing in your regrets, but being truly alive to all the possibilities wrapped up in this moment," his tone giving a particular emphasis to this moment.

Biting back my initial tendency to argue back I simply accepted his comment, returned from my reverie, and gave the rest of the workout my full attention.

"What's so great about that?" I can hear you ask, even if you noticed the last sentence at all? Well, for me it was huge. I didn't follow the usual pattern of arguing or defending myself or putting down his implied criticism with a cynical comment. I was changing, feeling more secure as a person.

When we finished our day's hike and got back to camp the afternoon after William's lecture, I attempted to distract William and hopefully start him in a different direction by asking him to show me how he had held me down the day after he had thrown the cup of water over me.

Instead of being a distraction, this was another of those pivotal moments that was the start of a whole new chapter in my life.

William said he had used a technique called *ikkyu* from the Japanese martial art aikido. Not only did he show me how to do it, but with his usual determination and enthusiasm, he insisted we practice it for nearly thirty minutes.

We cleaned up, lit a fire and had dinner. Afterward, I sprawled dejectedly in a folding camp chair, staring at the fire. I was feeling tired and melancholy. Without being able to put words to the feeling at the time, I guess I was wanting more from William than his emotional distance and endless training.

William, in an unusually perceptive moment, at least where I am concerned, realized I was feeling down and asked why. I didn't know what to say without sounding like I was blaming him.

"No particular reason, I'm just feeling tired of everything."

"I know that feeling well, but ultimately all the emotions we feel are a choice we make. I found meditation really helped me change what I felt and gave me a handle to control my emotions."

All my frustration at William's stoic impassivity burst out. "If I want to change I will get religion, and don't you dare assume you know me or what I feel. Don't presume to tell me what to do."

William was a little shocked by my vehemence but accepted it without rancor. Instead of the anger I had been feeling, I felt some sort of connection to him that was like a window to his heart. I could feel there was kindness behind his irritating words, but couldn't bring myself to say anything to break the silence.

"I apologize if I sounded pompous. I know I keep annoying you with my manner and I will change that if I can. If you would like me to explain what I meant about meditation, I will."

William offering to talk rather than me having to wheedle information was unusual enough for me to say without a second thought, "Please do."

"When I finished officer training and was given my first command I was so proud and full of myself. Being posted to Iraq quickly knocked all that out of me. Because I had received very high grades in every aspect of training and looked very good on paper, I was given command of an elite squad of Rangers. The problem being, there I was, out to prove myself and how good I was when in an all-out combat situation my training counted for nothing, and the experience of the men I commanded meant they were far more competent than me. They had to keep themselves alive while they waited for me, either to develop some healthy pragmatism and choose life or to get myself killed for some idiotic illusion of honor. If the latter happened, they would just have to go through the process all over again with the next green officer who replaced me. They were resigned to the process but still bitterly resented me for replacing a man they respected and trusted with their lives. He had gone home in several pieces after stepping on a mine.

"By the time we went into a major action together for the fourth time I had had my nose rubbed in reality enough to be working well with my squad. I was learning how to listen to their opinions without compromising my authority, and they trusted me enough to follow my orders without hesitation. I was feeling confident of our ability to handle our assignment, holding the market square that many of the twisted alleyways of the town opened into. We were spread over a couple of defensive positions on two adjacent sides of the square, our position blocking the movement and retreat of insurgents who were being forced out of their positions by other Ranger squads working down the streets toward us. However, the square was relatively large as it was a major market town so there was not enough good cover for my men. We were sporadically coming under heavy fire but returning much better than we got.

"At some point one of the wooden houses on the far side of the square was hit by a mortar or shell from a tank and caught on fire as part of it collapsed. A woman scrambled out over the wreckage carrying a baby. When she ran out into the square she was hit by a hail of bullets and—"

"It wasn't quite like that," I interrupted in a trance-like tone. "As soon as she was clear she began screaming and gesturing that there were children inside and begging for someone to help her save them. One of your men from the furthest position ran from behind the barricade to help her despite your order to stay down. As he reached her your enemies cut him down with a hail of automatic gunfire, not caring that they killed her too."

William whispered as the color drained from his face.

"You can't know that . . . but . . . how?"

"Yes, I can . . . and I do. I am seeing it all as if I am there too—no, that's not right, I think I am seeing it through your eyes. Anyway, you had to crouch there, safe behind your barricade but not able to do anything, while a man under your command died, the mother died and her children were burned alive."

William was more surprised than me and visibly disturbed. The pictures in my head disappeared as his concentration or confidence was shaken. He got up and walked off into the night with unshed tears shining in his eyes.

CHAPTER 9

ENTER THE DOJO

NEXT MORNING William was up as usual, and we followed our morning routine in silence, neither of us knowing how to deal with the implications of the previous night or willing to risk damaging the bond between us.

After breakfast William picked up the thread of last night's conversation seamlessly, as if there had been no interruption and nothing unusual had happened.

"Every man has a breaking point and I am no different. I had been in combat often enough by then to have come to terms as best I could with the images of battle—the specter of fear, hideous wounds and the screams of dying men. I had met all these and more on a regular basis and knew I would manage. But that day was different. I started having nightmares and doubting my decisions at crucial times. That's dangerous for anyone who has to rely on me."

I tried to console him. "It obviously wasn't your fault and there was nothing you could have done differently anyway." I knew from what I had seen and experienced from William's thoughts last night that he regarded the man who had tried to help as a friend and comrade, and felt his friend had had the courage to do what he should have done—to go to another's aid, regardless of the circumstances. As a result of his inability to help the people who had died, including his comrade and friend, he judged himself a coward and a failure even though he knew he had had no other choice.

"I know that," William stated emphatically, "and the shrinks at base told me that in a dozen different ways too. It didn't matter or help. I quickly realized, though, that I was going to have to do something about it for myself, before my squad lost confidence in me or I got myself killed or some worse disaster occurred."

"What do you mean worse than dying?"

"I'm not that afraid to die, but I would hate to be alive if my decisions— or rather, mistakes—were responsible for the death and suffering of other people. It would be hell living with that every day. So my troubled mind drifted back to meditation, something that had been included as part of my martial arts training.

"With no other option to deal with my troubles, I started regular meditation practice, or at least whenever I could get away with it. Meditation quickly increased my sensitivity to my inner mental states and I could see my emotions are a choice I am making. I found with practice I could see the triggers, the usually subconscious mental shifts that brought back particular emotions and their associated memories. If I was quick enough, I could change my focus and prevent myself falling into the depressive, helpless or self-pitying mental states that usually followed. Not that I'm saying it was easy—it wasn't."

William fell silent and wandered off to wash the dishes and I left him to it, feeling he wanted to be alone.

Rather than go hiking, William said he would like to move on to another place when he returned from the camp kitchen. We packed up our camp, putting the tents and gear into the car and drove off without any plan of where to go next. William just wanted to put the night's memories behind him. We made no mention of my mind-reading episode. Neither of us was ready to bring up the subject, too uncertain or scared of what the implications might be.

He stopped at the first town we came to, leaving me to go shopping at the supermarket while he disappeared into an Internet cafe for fifteen minutes, something he had not done before. He returned happily, and when I asked him what he had been up to he replied enigmatically, "You'll see."

We drove till the afternoon. He took us to a state forest park close to a large town where we set up our campsite as usual. Afterward we went walking hand in hand along a trail leading from the campground. When I suggested it was time to organize dinner he said, "Don't worry, I have something else in mind."

We waited till later in the evening, then William led me to the car and drove into the town. He handed me a map he had printed off the net and asked me to navigate, giving him warning of the turns to get to the address on the street he had marked.

His destination turned out to be a small aikido dojo, situated in an old industrial building in a run-down part of town. As we walked in William insisted I stop at the door and bow.

"You are committing yourself to leave outside all egotism and your emotional hang-ups, your bigotry. Enter with a pure heart. You are promising to respect the ways of the dojo because every dojo is different. If you are unhappy or disagree, then leave."

What stood out most for me from my first class was my clumsiness and ineptness as I tried the footwork and breakfall rolls for the first time. I was shown a couple of simple techniques too that seemed easy to explain but absurdly hard to execute when having to move both hands, both feet and respond to my partner in unfamiliar ways all at once.

After the session, we drove to a late-night café. As we ate our dinner William was bubbling over with enthusiasm and talked almost non-stop; he was silent only when getting the food into his mouth. He had not trained for a long time and was overjoyed to be back on the mat. I was enjoying seeing him being so animated, so when he asked what I thought I replied, "I guess everybody needs a hobby."

William was scandalized.

"A *hobby*," he echoed incredulously. "It's not a hobby; it's a way of life."

To be honest, although I had felt like the uncoordinated new-born foal I had once seen trying to stand up, the beauty of the art had enthralled me as I had watched the higher grades training, but I was not in a hurry to tell

William that. He was always so straightforward and down to earth he never noticed when he was being wound up and I was enjoying his discomfort.

I finally broke out in giggles at his intensity and he glared at me as comprehension dawned.

"All right," he said finally, "that's another one I owe you."

– CHAPTER 10 –

OUT OF THE FRYING PAN

WILLIAM DECIDED to stay at the camp for the time being and we went to the aikido club whenever they were training, organizing our days around their schedule.

When we were training at the dojo a few days later, the sensei took the beginners, me and Trevor, aside on the mat to talk to us. Trevor had been coming for a few weeks so had a far better idea of what he was doing than I had. He was big and muscular with a strong competitive streak. I had noticed Sensei Adrian Monteith watching and talking to Trevor occasionally last class as well, but now he wanted him to think about why his initial reaction was always to resist other people and try to prove he was better.

"Aikido is practiced through cooperation between people, never competition," the instructor said. "To really understand it you need to get past the attack–defend, winner–loser, survivor–lunch dichotomy that is hard wired into our biology. If all you want is to defend yourself, buy a gun, it's easier and quicker. If you want to take this seriously, start looking at all the ways you react violently to any situation. When you need to be smarter, prettier, wealthier than other people, you are seeing the world from a violent perspective, always in opposition to the world around you. Aikido says to get out of the way of conflict and then blend with attacks to neutralize them. The intent is not to destroy. What makes aikido unique is that it is a cooperative martial art where people progress through helping each other learn rather than by defeating each other."

He had obviously had enough of Trevor's attitude.

"If you just want to fight you should choose another martial art."

As I watched William with some of the higher grades throwing each other around at the other end of the mat it didn't look very peaceful, so I asked William about it later that night at our campsite.

"Learning to do our techniques with more power and speed is obviously important in many ways, but what's really important is internal. Being balanced, centered and grounded—having your mind fully present in your body and in time while you move—is far more important and much harder to achieve. This is what you carry with you every minute into whatever you do. To be honest, if you can achieve it, it makes you far more effective as a martial artist too."

While William was talking I noticed that in some way I was aware of what he was meaning rather than just hearing and interpreting his words. I realized over the last few days that the empathetic link between us was growing stronger. I was increasingly aware of how he was feeling, but made the mistake of not telling him.

It was almost a week since he had opened up and since then he had returned to his silent, taciturn self. Eventually, after some not so subtle emotional blackmail, he agreed to continue.

"The attack at Mosul happened almost a year later and by then my mental focus or control was so sharp, the idea of self-doubt seemed ridiculous. I had practiced karate and boxing while I was at school and pushed myself relentlessly. As I look back now, I know I was trying to make myself into the man my father never was and that I guess I hated him for not being. I had approached meditation with the same ruthless fanaticism and devoted any spare moment I had to it in one form or another. Even so, I was completely taken by surprise by what happened.

"I didn't know where I was when I got home to the US. The doctor assigned to me for the trip had tried to sedate me when we first landed, but the needle only bent on my skin. One of the four butch MPs accompanying me made a call, after which they blindfolded and handcuffed me before handing me over to a new group of troglodytes who moved me on to my final destination.

"I was locked in a room beside the medical center, which was really a research lab. They thoughtfully put an armed guard outside to usher me to wherever I had to go. I was put through a battery of physical tests and all they showed was that I was effectively invulnerable. Some of the tests themselves should have been terrifying, but I had this unshakable certainty that I could not be harmed.

"I only ever saw one doctor, Brian, who conducted the tests, and a psychologist, who called himself Alan, and kept asking me random questions. Alan often visited me in my room too and continued our conversations. The other person present each time was a nurse-technician who efficiently set up the experiments.

"Whenever they were going to do anything particularly nasty to me, like the time they had a laser set up when I was brought in and tried firing that at me, the nurse would strap me in to a mechanized examination table that would move me into whatever position they wanted while it restrained me. On one occasion, the nurse passed her hand over my eyes, showing a small scrap of folded paper hidden in her palm. I felt her hand in my pocket a little later as she was putting on the side straps.

"I read her note in my room. 'Don't give up hope. There are others like you. We will help you if we can.' It had never occurred to me that I could or should give up hope.

"A day or two after, the psychologist asked me why I had never tried to get out of the straps. 'Why should I?' I replied. 'It makes no difference to me.'"

"He said, 'Humor me for a moment and try to get out.' I extended or tensed my will rather than my body and the restraints snapped as my arms moved, without me even noticing their resistance. As I didn't enjoy being tied down I moved on to tearing the examination table apart, including its steel frame, partly out of interest to see if I could.

"I stopped when I heard Alan cough behind me and say, 'Yes, I think that will be enough, thank you.' I turned to see the others had all backed away including my loyal shadow, who had his M16 at his shoulder sighted on me. I looked at him and politely said, 'I have been hit from larger weapons than that and it made no difference, so you might as well put it down.' I was actually trying to put him at his ease, but I suspect the fact that I was still absentmindedly holding a thirty-inch-long piece of two-by-two box section from the table frame in my right hand didn't help. They all reacted as if it was a threat and though nobody moved, the involuntary stiffening and the look in their eyes showed that where they had been afraid before, they were terrified now. The doctor was starting to visibly shake.

"I realized that with their restraints and the armed guard they had felt powerful and safe but now, knowing they were helpless and weak, and no doubt remembering some of the awful things they had done to me and to god knows how many others too, they were ready to panic—reacting to their own feelings of guilt and the fear of retribution as much as their present fear of me."

I asked William, "But why was Odette so scared too? If she was on your side, she should have been happy to see you free yourself."

William paused and after a moment asked me warily, "What do you mean?"

I blithely continued. "Her face, it's gone white and her mouth is hanging slightly open. From the way she is trying to melt into the wall behind her it is clear she is as terrified as the others. I can see it in your head."

I couldn't have said anything worse at that moment. I could feel an icy rage building up in William.

"I don't want you in my head; I don't want anyone in my head. I don't want you anywhere near me. You are just like him, aren't you?"

He started to walk off, then turned on his heel and threw the car keys to me. They hit me on the chest and bounced off into the night. I numbly watched William walk to his tent, throw his meager belongings into his pack and stride down the driveway into the night. To me it seemed he was dwarfed by the giant specter of rage that walked in his shoes.

– CHAPTER 11 –

NOT AGAIN . . .

I GOT UP LATE and found the keys where they had fallen the night before. I know I'm supposed to shrug it off and take positive self-empowering action to change the situation. Bollocks. I sat and waited, hoping he would come back and at the same time knowing he would not. When, at the end of the day, I finally accepted the inevitable. I threw the tents and my stuff into the back of the car and drove off.

I left feeling grief—grief for me, grief for William, grief for the dojo who had treated us like family that I was leaving without a goodbye. I even avoided the town with its happy memories and took the long way to the interstate so I wouldn't have to drive through it. I decided it was time to do something for my peace of mind and aching heart and drove seventy-five miles to the nearest large city. After filling up with petrol, I drove across the street to a 7-Eleven and bought the essential ingredients to my plan, a book and two bottles, one of wine, the other of bubble-bath. I stopped at the first large motel that took my fancy and said I want a large bath, and a quiet room away from the road to go with it.

I spent most of the night in hot water and finished the wine and the book in that order. I finally crawled off to bed, not feeling good, but at least resigned and more peaceful. Waking next morning wasn't so pretty, but I survived the experience and promptly went back to sleep to try to forget it.

I finally got up and took a bus into the CBD for the afternoon, so I didn't have to worry about parking the car or driving on the wrong side of the road in an unfamiliar city. If it had been earlier I would have looked for a museum or something, but settled for walking the streets looking at the sights and moping. I passed a movie theatre and on impulse went in and watched the next feature. When I left the theater, I walked back the way I had come, trying desperately to remember the bus stop location so I could get back to the hotel. I came to a nightclub that I had passed earlier. I went in, got a drink and sat on a stool by the wall so I would only get hemmed in on one side. I love to dance; moving makes me feel good and I was just waiting for the dance floor to fill up so I could dance on my own in anonymity.

I sat for a while when the insidious thought *I can't imagine William dancing* crossed my mind and I was feeling terrible again. It took a while but when the floor started to fill I joined in that ancient rite of happiness and forgetting.

I walked out feeling alive again and very nearly experienced the opposite. It was late now, and I was looking to find a taxi back to the hotel. I should have gone back inside and asked them to call me one, but I walked down the street, hoping one would pass by. I was following two young men on the sidewalk. As they reached the end of the block a huge guy walked around the corner from the side street and almost walked into them. They stopped so close they could have touched but stopped dead rather than walking around each other. There was a cold, tense silence, but the big man was obviously feeling confident.

He sneered at the other two and when neither moved he said, "Do your mommas know you're out of bed?"

One of the boys made a terse reply I missed as he was facing away from me.

The big guy just laughed.

"Go home to your teddy bear, kid."

This was too much for the man addressed as kid. He twitched and a switchblade appeared in his hand. He was obviously well practiced with the movement. A gun appeared in the big man's hand. He could have shot both of them but was only intending to scare them off. After a moment's standoff, Switchblade's friend grabbed at the big man's arm, pushing the gun sideways. It fired, shattering the silence of the night. Switchblade leapt in and stabbed the big guy several times, once in the arm his friend was clinging to, causing the gun to fall to the street. The big man slowly fell.

Switchblade and his friend stood staring at the fallen man.

"We got to go," Switchblade said. He looked over his shoulder as he stepped around the body, saw me and said, "Aw fuck . . . She knows who we are, you'll have to kill her."

"Screw you, do it yourself if you want," Switchblade's friend said.

"I'm sorry, girl, it's not my fault," Switchblade said, picking up the gun and pointing it at me.

"It is your fault," I said. "You didn't have to do any of this and you are wrong about me knowing who you are, too. I don't have a clue."

Switchblade grabbed my arm with his free hand and said to his friend, "Help me with her, we'll take her with us and Carlos can sort it out."

They held an arm each, but I walked between them with as much dignity as I could, I didn't want to be dragged, and I was feeling nauseous. I got in their car, as there was no point arguing with an idiot holding a gun. I didn't want to give them the idea I was more trouble than I was worth.

We drove for what must have been less than ten minutes with Switchblade glaring at me from the far side of the back seat. They took me into a tidy, sprawling two-story house in a quiet backstreet. After they hammered on the door, the two hulking hired help who appeared in answer escorted us into a room where a well-dressed man sat at a desk in a large, imposing black leather chair.

"How dare you come to my home at this time of night," Carlos said. "And who in the hell is that?"

Stung by his comment I said, "Cool chair, bro, did your mum give it to you?"

Switchblade's friend gave him a story of their epic struggle when the man with the gun, apparently named Dimitri, ruthlessly attacked them.

Carlos growled. "Madre Dios, we are losing territory to Ivan's gangs as it is. The last thing we need is a gang war because you idiots killed his son. You did kill him, didn't you?"

Switchblade volunteered that they hadn't checked if he was dead, so they had no idea.

Carlos pulled open a drawer in his desk and handed Switchblade a cell phone.

"Get away from here then phone the cops and tell them you saw someone stabbed and where. Then get rid of the phone and keep way from here until I contact you."

Switchblade slunk out the door with the phone still in his hand.

Carlos turned to the other boy and snarled "Juan, get her in there," indicating a door opposite the one we had come through, "and keep her quiet. I'm expecting the deputy commissioner and haven't time to clean up after you."

It was a small room sparsely furnished with a bed and an easy chair. Carlos obviously used it when he was working and didn't want to leave his office area. Juan closed the door, made me sit on the bed and lazed back in the chair and started playing with his knife while staring at me.

"Don't make a noise, girly, or I will use this on you," he said as he flourished the knife. I'll say this for him, he was awfully brave and manly when he had a helpless victim in front of him who wasn't in a position to fight back.

It must have been hours before the deputy commissioner came and went. I could hear some of the conversation through the door and it was clear Carlos was arranging to pay him off for some favor and was negotiating the terms. Carlos took him somewhere else in the house for almost an hour, and when they returned both men were laughing. Part payment in advance apparently made the atmosphere much more cordial.

The deputy commissioner left shortly after and dread filled my mind as I expected Carlos to call us in and seal my fate. I heard a very faint noise after he left, and then silence again. A few minutes later I heard the door burst open from the passage into Carlos' room and the commissioner saying angrily, "What the hell is this about?"

There was a short silence and I was stunned to hear William's voice saying coldly, "Apparently you know where my girlfriend is."

Carlos replied carefully, "What if I do?"

There was silence for a short time then William said, "I will count to five . . . one . . . two . . ."

On three Carlos lost his nerve and yelled, "Juan, bring the girl in."

Juan grabbed my arm and jerked me off the bed. He stepped behind me, put his left arm around my chest to hold me and held the knife to my throat with his other hand. When we got to the door he ordered, "Open it, but don't say anything."

As we stepped through the door locked together, Juan turned us so I was between Juan and the door to the corridor where he was expecting William to be. But William had moved to beside Carlos's desk where he had his back to a wall with a clear view of both doors while still holding the commissioner with one hand by the scruff of his jacket.

Juan was holding the knife lightly to my throat but had his back to William. He started to move around me to his right so he could see both of us and keep the knife at my throat at the same time. William was staring directly at me and smiling. He winked at me, then coughed and shrugged his shoulders as if tensing to act. A ripple went through the room as all the attention focused back on him. Juan turned his head slightly too and as he did I flung my left arm up and outwards, hitting his right arm to push the knife away from my throat and stepped in to hit him as hard as I could in the throat. I know it's not ladylike but I'm not stupid enough to want to break my fingers on his jaw. As the punch connected I pushed hard on him with both hands and jumped back in case he slashed back with the knife. He didn't, reeling back gagging while I hit the frame of the door he had just pulled me through with one shoulder and fell over in the doorway. Not the look I was wanting at all.

As I stumbled to my feet, Juan fell back toward William who spun him by the shoulder, jerked his wrist back and removed the knife then dropped him to the ground in a single smooth movement with an elbow to the jaw. Carlos had jerked a drawer open in his desk and was still trying to pull a gun out of it as William spun a swinging back kick that slammed it closed against his hand. The commissioner was pulling a gun from a shoulder holster as William gripped his arm and swung it over to lock his elbow, forcing him to drop the gun. William then threw him to the ground where he sprawled limply.

It was over in seconds as William picked up the gun and faced Carlos who was cradling his smashed hand. He stepped around the desk and took Carlos's gun from the drawer, then stepped back with a gun in each of his hands.

Damn it all. Here was his big chance to sweep me off my feet and profess his undying devotion to me and what happens? He was standing in the midst of mayhem, a gun in each hand with two dead or unconscious bodies on the floor, but the best he could come up with was "Okay, at this stage I have lost count of the number of times I have walked away from you and it would be most unbecoming of you to remind me so let's not go there, please," he finished sheepishly.

I looked at him as the silence stretched and I finally understood what he was feeling. He would happily face death without blinking an eye. Attacking armed men empty handed and rescuing damsels in distress, all in a day's work. But standing there in front of me, he seemed desperately shy and vulnerable. He didn't have fifteen years of training telling him how to deal with personal situations like this.

"Coward," I yelled. He tried to squeeze in the word "Absolutely" as I stormed toward him saying, "Idiot." He went to step back to avoid me, but I grabbed him, hugging him like it was the end of the world, then pulled his head down and kissed him. As usual when something is really important, I had to organize it all.

A little later I asked, "Why, William?" He checked the safety on each gun and put them in his pockets.

"It seems you are in my head whether I want it or not," he smiled wryly. "I could feel you were in desperate trouble and could even tell in which direction I had to go. I grabbed a cab straight away and kept going till somewhere around here. I randomly knocked on a few doors and said or yelled depending on what the situation suggested something along the lines of 'What have you done with my girlfriend?' This was the first house where I got a positive response. The rest is history," he said. "However, there are a lot of very confused people around here just now."

He turned back to glare at Carlos, who had clearly thought better of moving, sighed, then said, "Let's go."

– CHAPTER 12 –

A PROMISE MADE

We walked out of the house and down the drive hand in hand, stepping around the limp form of one of Carlos's troll-like employees. William smiled and said, "He did not want to tell me where you were and, sadly, I had to throw him over the car while we were debating the issue. Unfortunately, his *ukemi* was not up to it, but on the bright side," he added wryly, "the deputy commissioner became very keen to show me how to find Carlos and maybe you at that point." William paused to leave the two guns in the letterbox.

As we walked down the quiet suburban avenue, William put his arm around my shoulder so I stepped around in front of him, stopping him in his tracks and demanded, "Since when have I been your girlfriend?"

"Some things are just so obvious," he said. "Why would you question fate?"

"But you are supposed to ask me," I countered.

"Okay, consider yourself asked." He turned me around, put his arm around me and dragged me along with the sheer force of his overwhelming confidence.

We called a cab and got a ride back to an all-night café near the hotel. We ordered coffee and William got something to eat as well. We were working through our second or third refill as the night turned toward morning when William yawned, stretched and asked, "Where do we go from here?"

I tilted my head a little to the side, raised my eyebrows and said sweetly, "Do you need me to draw you a map, William?"

The effect was wonderful. William flushed pink and choked on his coffee, trying vainly to hold back coughs as he fought to regain his composure. He was almost there when I continued, "Once again your silver tongue and smooth *savoir faire* has turned me to putty in your hands," which started him off choking again. I couldn't keep a straight face and started giggling, which quickly degenerated to me collapsing into fits of hysterical laughter as the terror and disappointment of the last twenty-four hours ebbed.

William caught his breath and tried to look dignified, which only made it worse for me, but the façade began to crack and soon he was laughing uncontrollably too.

As we finally pulled ourselves together and wiped our eyes, William sobered up.

"You know that's not what I meant. I want to apologize to you and for you to understand where you stand with me, because my behavior toward you has not always been reasonable and, given time, I will explain some more of my experiences as best I can. All I want to say about it right now is that sometimes I am reacting to feelings and memories I would rather were forgotten but still haunt me.

"What I mean to say is the only thing I can offer you, and to me it is the most valuable thing I own, my solemn word of honor. A promise if you want to think of it that way, but it means much more to me than that. I will stand by you and be there for you if you need me. I will never walk out on you again."

We sat for some time in that warm, encompassing silence that needs no explanations. "Thank you, William, I accept." I took his hand and we walked out of the café into the night.

CHAPTER 13

BACK TO THE TREADMILL

WE GOT UP LATE the next morning and mooched around the city. As William had no plans or things to do and no doubt was still feeling guilty too, he docilely followed me around through an art gallery and a museum. However, between the two, he ducked into an Internet café and printed out the contact details for all the dojos in the area. He was much happier for the rest of the day while I sighed to myself knowing my evenings—and probably mornings—were being organized for some indefinite time into the future.

Accepting the inevitable, I went with him to training that evening. It's always interesting going to a new dojo. You might be doing the same things, but the perspective is always different and there is always something new to learn.

Because I was a beginner everyone tolerated my idiosyncrasies and corrected them cheerfully. William was not so lucky. A short while after we started our third technique for the evening, his black-belt partner yelled, "You're just treating me like a piece of meat," and stormed off the mat. William stood bemused for a moment before one of the other black-belts called him over to their group and he continued training.

I asked William about the incident over dinner later and he brushed over it saying he had no idea what was behind the outburst.

"I need to figure out what is going on with your mind reading because I am extremely sensitive to people stamping their hobnail boots through my head. I can't be at ease around you until I know what is going on. Would you help me with figuring it out, please?"

I assented, to which he replied, "That's good, we'll start tomorrow," and stood up to leave.

Next day we started back on our earlier routine, though we had to find city parks to run in, and then started on exploring the link between us. Over the next few days we figured out that the link was strongest when we were both relaxed but fully focused and paying attention. Most importantly, with practice William was able to tell when I was seeing what he was seeing and control it. He felt able to drop his guard around me again and continued talking about his experiences.

"After a day or two, the doctor got tired of bending his needles on my skin and giving me drugs that had no effect, so I had my first visit from Argus. I was escorted to a briefing room and after he introduced himself, we sat across from each other around a table and had a friendly, superficial conversation. At the same time, I could sense him trying to affect my mind, to find some way of controlling it or seeing into it but his efforts seemed ridiculous. He tried again the next day with the same results, then left me alone for a while.

"By that time too, word of the results of the tests on me had got back to General Ryder, the Army officer in charge of this particular clandestine operation. When he heard what I could do he thought he had hit the jackpot. With a small army of invulnerable soldiers, you could control the world. He came to the base immediately and I was escorted to meet him in the experimental lab with the doctor and psychologist present. We looked each other over in silence, then he introduced himself rather than waiting for someone to do so. It was less of an introduction and more his taking control of the situation with the calm assurance of someone long used to absolute command. He stood slightly over average height with a body that was obviously in perfect condition despite the age and experience suggested by the many medal ribbons and the stars on his shoulders. It was obvious he was very careful about his appearance but the untinted grey in his close-cropped hair told me vanity was not the reason. After sizing me up he gazed casually at the doctor and snapped, 'Get on with it.' Clearly politeness was only wasted on his superiors. He watched the demonstrations impassively but there was a veneer of obvious satisfaction that flickered over his face. The doctor ordered my minder to shoot me with his assault rifle, and it had no effect.

"The general made immediate arrangements to get some influential people, including scientists, to come to the base and the doctors and I set up the demonstration."

William had been calmly focused on communicating the story completely and as he felt the link form between our minds, stopped talking, but continued to recount the events in his mind.

I could sense the change in his mind as he decided to stop the flow. It was like a wall instantly went up between us as the link was broken. He then asked me to tell him the story back, which I could as if I had experienced it myself. When I had finished he smiled and commented, "That was interesting," and left it at that.

Personally, I thought it was amazing.

Next time we were at the dojo, the senior sensei was teaching the basic form of the technique William had supposedly been doing wrong on our first night there. He made it very clear that if you didn't do it his way you were treating your partner like a "piece of meat." I couldn't help thinking, as a beginner and having already been in several dojos that sometimes taught the same techniques in quite different ways, how incredibly arrogant it was to make such sweeping statements, to think you could judge other people's intentions in such a blanket manner.

I later asked William what he thought about it.

"Dojo myths are often created when a sensei makes comments or metaphors as a way of getting an idea across that are then taken as a literal fact by their students. On the other hand, there are sensei who are every bit as arrogant and blind as you can imagine." He laughed. "To be honest, I see their point and agree the way they do that technique is better, in some respects, but think about it. I hurt that guy because he resisted what I was doing and gave no indication that I was hurting him. He was so intent on proving his superiority and showing I was doing it wrong, he didn't do what even a paramecium, a brainless single cell, will do. Move away from or react to pain." As I was looking blank he snorted again, "The guy actually behaved as if he was a dead 'piece of meat.'"

William went silent for a while, so I asked him what happened after the demonstration for the scientists and the others.

"I was an overnight sensation. They wanted to reproduce the effect in other soldiers and I was the one supposed to make it happen, but in the frame of mind I was in, I couldn't see the point or, rather, I didn't agree with their motives.

"The doctor and psychologist decided the effects came in some way from my unshakable knowledge or awareness that I could not be harmed. They called in some extra psychologists and other specialists. Along with them came a flock of support staff—technicians and nurses and equipment like EEGs, biofeedback monitors and the like. With the general's help they had a willing group of *volunteers* within three days. They started to experiment with mixtures of drugs and hypnosis to see if they could induce in test subjects the changes in their core beliefs that would allow them to develop similar abilities to those I demonstrated.

"It took more days to get them imprinted to the level the experts wanted. The men truly believed they were invulnerable, but the effect was very different, depending on the individual character of the men. The conflict between their deep beliefs, their instinctual, survival reflexes really, and the imprinting of new opposing commands over the top produced psychosis and highly unpredictable results.

"Why do we behave acceptably in our societies? If our only motivation is fear of the consequences, the retaliation or revenge that society or police will exact for infringements of the social or legal laws, what happens when people believe they are invulnerable? The programming had different results depending on the psychology of the person but on some it removed all the inhibitions against self-indulgence and violence. One soldier, who was normally a decent enough person, tried to rape one of the nurses he had been friendly with before he even got to do any tests. It was only through the intervention of two of the other conditioned men that she was saved, although she was badly beaten. Neither he nor the nurse were seen again in the compound. All female personnel were removed from the program after this and one or two other incidents.

"A big part of the conditioning had also been to obey orders from superiors as the thought of a group of invulnerable, free-willed soldiers roaming the country was anathema to the general, the type of man who saw domination of others as his natural right.

"Most of the men would follow any order, even if it meant obvious suicide to a rational man, but there was still subconscious conflict. One became catatonic when ordered to kill another. He didn't know the gun was loaded with blanks. In general, the men showed much more strength than usual but had no concepts of their usual limits. They could kill or injure themselves doing things that weren't particularly dangerous because they didn't feel the need to take the usual amount of care. They did feel or believe they were invulnerable, but they never were.

"All the attempts were disastrous and unfortunately left a group of dead and severely damaged young men, both physically and psychologically. It says something about the general's attitude that only men had been chosen to take part."

CHAPTER 14

EYE OF THE HURRICANE

After General Ryder's first visit, William was treated with a little more respect. For a short time, he became somewhat of a celebrity prisoner as the general wanted him to act as his ambassador in selling this breakthrough to his superiors. William was released from his cell and given a room at ground level in another building in the compound. He was happy for two reasons: one, he could see the sun again and, two, there were other inmates, other people who had shown unusual talents, he could talk to.

Odette was the first to welcome him to his new home. She walked up and gave William a warm hug as she whispered into his ear, "We are under surveillance here at all times of course, so think carefully before you speak." She introduced him to the few people who were there, and it was quite obvious from their comments she had already told them all about his abilities.

After she had given him a tour of their boundaries, she took him to their mess hall, poured hot drinks for them both and led him back out to sit on a bench in the warm morning sun.

"The people you see here are the ones who are not regarded as potentially dangerous. Hank Lee, the tall guy with the beard, was in an APC with a squad of soldiers when he suddenly ordered them to get out and hit the dirt. Seconds later it was destroyed by a rogue missile. It turned out he shows some precognition, he sees what is going to happen before it happens. They tested him in all the usual sorts of ways, things like predicting which number a dice will roll or what card will turn up next, and he is statistically consistent. What that means is that he is right more often than he should be, but you can't make military decisions on the assumption that he is right a little more often than chance says he can be."

Odette stopped, pointed to a man walking out of the nearest building and said, "Kenji, there is another interesting one." Then she yelled "Hey Kenji, get your butt over here."

Kenji ambled over and greeted Odette with a hug as she stood up to meet him. He shook hands with William as Odette introduced them and she asked him to tell his story.

Kenji grinned and said, "I'm guessing she means the incident that brought me here, so I won't bore you with my life history.

"I was one of six soldiers on perimeter sentry duty during the night for a long-distance field operation that saw us camped out in the mountains. There were two of us each in three camouflaged positions making a triangle a couple of hundred yards out from the camp. There was no base close enough to the objective, a rebel military stronghold, where we could assemble our armored ground force, so we had assembled in the desert at a distance intelligence had decided would not compromise our attack the following day. We were supposed to go in around ten a.m. following an air strike.

"I had the watch after midnight and within minutes of being left in my position started seeing enemy fighters approaching in old four-wheel drives. It was dark, but I still could see the men and their vehicles clearly in my mind's eye. There was no sign of any enemy in the night, but I became absolutely convinced what I was seeing was real and called in for the force commander to be woken up. When the lieutenant on com duty at the camp laughed and told me to stop being an idiot I said I would go to his tent and wake him myself if I had to. As I would be court martialed for leaving my post the operator gave orders for the major to be called but made it clear it was on my head, not his.

"The major sent another soldier to relieve me and turned on me as I ducked my head and entered the command tent. Walking into the dull light in the tent and being met by the full force of his anger and disbelief caused me to lose the thread of what I was seeing. However, by this time I was certain the men were coming on what was little more than a side trail over another pass in the mountains that joined the main road a little ahead of us. They would be here in time to hit us while it was still dark, before the sun rose in the morning. After some arguing, when I was still adamant in the face of his hostility and threats, the major woke the force and spread the troops out in hidden positions away from the camp. I was left with the other soldiers in the sentry positions along with a minimum of soldiers in the camp to make it look inhabited."

Kenji paused, saying, "You have finished your coffees and I need one after talking so much so I'm going to get myself one and you can refill yours yourself if you want." William and Odette followed him back into the building.

They returned with brimming mugs and I could still feel the joy in William's memory as he walked out into the sunlight again. He hated being confined indoors. William sat peacefully while Odette and Kenji gossiped about others who had come and gone. William asked why they were still there, effectively held prisoner in a secret enclave.

"I have seen too much in the labs for the general to be happy for me to be released," Odette said, "and, like Kenji and Hank, I'm still useful."

His question had turned their mood serious again and Kenji said, "I'd better finish my story as I've got work to do. We waited with radios on and continued making our scheduled calls in but were ordered to make no move until we got the order to go from command. The attackers crept as close as they could in their vehicles, but stopped three or four miles away to avoid any noise that would give them away. They obviously had some intelligence about the camp, probably a spy on the distant hills with a telescope watching us when we set up camp in the evening, as they split into two groups that moved silently between the sentry positions. The attack was well coordinated as three groups of two men each waited behind and slithered toward the sentry positions while the two main groups paused to set up weapons. The other sentries and I were getting extremely jumpy as we had been issued night vision glasses and could see the attackers sneaking up on us but were not to respond until ordered. We were not helpless as our positions were slightly dug in and we could drop into cover if we had to but that would let them know we knew they were there. We were keeping their attention like ducks in the crosshairs at a carnival show.

"They had obviously decided not to use their guns on us as they were getting close enough to lob grenades into our foxholes when the major finally gave those of us near the camp the order to open fire. The insurgents were caught by surprise and ran to withdraw in the face of heavy fire, leaving behind the heavy tank killers they were putting together. Their trucks rushed to meet them as they retreated. They had intended to make a lightning strike, disable as much of our heavy armor and vehicles as they could while their drivers were to come in as the attack started, pick them up, then escape into the hills before we could organize our counter attack. The trucks ran into our forward positions and were destroyed by grenade launchers and heavy fire. Some of the attackers vanished into the desert night, but the majority either surrendered or were already numbered among the casualties.

"The major reviewed the situation and decided that, as the attack was aimed at the vehicles and as they seemed desperate to delay us, he would move out immediately. I did not see the rest of the fighting though as he left me behind, along with a small squad of men to guard the prisoners and tend our own wounded, until the column returned. I don't know if this was intended as a commendation or a reprimand."

He finished, looking at his watch. "We'll talk again later," and walked off quickly.

William was mostly left to his own devices over the next few days. Odette was kept very busy overseeing all the little administrative tasks for the medical and psychological tests on the guinea pigs as well as being called on to serve as a technician or nurse if one was not available. William spent most of his time alone, not exactly thinking about but more experiencing what was to him a completely new and alien way of living in the world, one that was utterly peaceful.

Odette and William spent an increasing amount of time in each other's company after she was removed from General Ryder's project. William asked her one day why she was there. She laughed happily and said, "What kind of weird psychic weapon would you expect a nurse to develop?"

"I don't know," William answered. "Did you kill all your patients?"

She laughed again but with more than a tinge of irony this time.

"No, stupid," she exclaimed, "sometimes I heal people. How threatening is that?"

She continued. "I was stationed at a field hospital and left to watch over a badly wounded man who would undoubtedly die during the night. Against all possible odds he not only survived the night but showed a major improvement in his condition and continued to improve after he was evacuated out to a base hospital. The doctor in charge thought it strange enough to write a report and somebody was sent to check to see if we had accidently done something that could help other soldiers in the same state. He decided almost immediately we hadn't done anything unusual and had some spare time before returning to his base. With nothing to do he looked over our records with a statistics program to see how our success rates measured up to other, similar field hospitals. Our overall success rate was significantly better than average, so when he looked into it more closely he discovered that wounded men had a better chance of survival or a faster recovery if I was their primary care-giver. It interested him enough to check records at my last posting after he left us, and the same result showed up. He sent in his own report and it twisted its way through the labyrinthine military maze of misinformation. Six months later, I was peremptorily summoned here."

William asked her if she had learned how to control and improve her abilities. She sighed.

"No, and the opposite usually happens when people are brought here. No one but Argus has developed much to my knowledge. For all of us, the attempt to control or bend something that is not part of our reasoning, conscious mind to our personal will seems to erode the ability over time.

"A common factor in many of the events seems to be the people were concerned about more than just themselves. A depth of goodwill and care seems to be part of the formula. When we come here to the hostility of the good doctor and his kindred spirits, and also come to see that this program is devoted to developing new weapons, or at the very least new forms of control, our own humanity or hope or optimism, I don't know which, is ground down in the face of it."

When Odette told William what she had uncovered about how ruthlessly the young men who had volunteered for the good of their country were being treated, he was appalled.

Cracks were starting to appear around the edges of William's perfect personal paradise.

– CHAPTER 15 –

FALL FROM GRACE

GENERAL RYDER was visiting regularly as he had a great deal riding on the success of his current project. Odette told William the Prometheus Project had been running for many years, but so far, while there had been one or two successes with soldiers reliably wielding special abilities, mostly results seemed to be random. Pressure to perform caused people to lose any gifts they showed more often than not. General Ryder was equally under pressure from his own superiors to show something valuable enough to justify the continued expense of maintaining the secret facility.

Two days later William was ushered into an office where the general sat commandingly in a high-backed antique armchair behind a large mahogany desk. He gestured perfunctorily for William to sit in the simple chair opposite him. He stared dismissively at William for long enough to establish his dominance.

"Well?" General Ryder acted as if William was personally responsible for the failure of his latest attempt to produce the perfect weapon. After another silence he grated, "If you don't have anything to add that might help the success of my project, get out and don't waste my time."

William calmly replied, "You will achieve nothing by continuing to experiment on those men. You are wasting their lives needlessly. In fact, you cannot even understand why your attitude, your state of mind, makes it impossible for you to ever succeed. You have to stop."

General Ryder bristled at what he saw as contempt of his authority. How dare William speak to him in that way. He looked William steadily in the eye and said in measured tones, "Don't tell me what I have to do. Here, my word is law. I may not be able to harm you, but I can lock you up for the rest of your life. It is time you cooperated with me or, believe me, I will find a way to make you suffer."

William looked at him calmly.

"I have cooperated, otherwise I would not still be here. I could have walked out any time I chose. None of your walls can stop me, none of your weapons can hurt me."

General Ryder gazed at William, in fact he leaned over the desk to stare straight into William's eyes as he reveled in his power.

"You have such pretty sisters. There are people out there who do such terrible things to girls like that. Sometimes the cruelest thing they do is to leave their victims alive afterwards. Would that hurt you, William? Your mother still lives in your old home, doesn't she? I hope she stays well. And then there's your young brother, I hear he is doing well in college. I would hate to even suggest what accidents could befall such a promising young man. If you look carefully, I think you will see you are wrong when you say I am not able to hurt you.

"As to you thinking you are invulnerable, I am intrigued to see what a tactical nuke would do to you. It would be a shame about all the casualties around you. However, we do have to put up with some collateral damage in the interests of progress, and besides, it would be a terrorist attack anyway, so what can you expect?"

Their gazes locked, and neither could look away. William looked deep into the general's soul and could not see a trace of pity or compassion. Beneath the civilized veneer all William could see was the urge to dominate and rule. Power was all that mattered, and worse than that was the desire, savage to the point of insanity, to rend and destroy anything that could not be controlled. Behind what seemed only a small and insignificant man, a vast hatred and rage for anything that stood in its way stalked hand in hand with that insatiable lust for power, all controlled and hidden behind his carefully cultivated image of reason and service to his country.

William knew then, as he struggled to free himself, that demons can walk the Earth in the shape of men.

For the first time in nearly a month, William was afraid—not for himself or his safety, but for the people he loved and all those others that this man would unhesitatingly and unthinkingly destroy without a qualm to achieve any end he thought important. William even felt fear or pity for General Ryder.

William had shown a great deal of reluctance to tell me about his meeting with the general. He said he would skip it as it brought back too many vile memories. It took two days before he relented. I did not want to force him, but I knew instinctively it was too important to pass over. Although he had really intended to keep this part of his story verbal, by the time he and General Ryder broke their deadlock and both looked away together, I was there too, as if in the room with them.

I saw through William's eyes as he staggered to his feet.

"I understand you now," William said.

General Ryder replied with steel still in his voice, though he was clearly just as shaken, "Yes, you do," completely missing what William had been referring to. He made no move or comment as William walked to the door and exited.

At this stage William was like an innocent. He had not needed all the barriers the rest of us have carefully constructed in our minds to shut out or at least strike a compromise with our fears and insecurities. The mental defenses we take for granted had been left behind.

William was completely engulfed by fear. He ran to his room, slamming the door and barricading it by sliding the small desk and his bed against it, as locks would have implied a privacy that was not tolerated in the compound.

If you have ever lived knowing the next knock at the door might be the secret police, come to take you away to torture, humiliation and certain death, knowing it will happen but never knowing when the ax will fall; if you have walked a secluded path, alone in the dark of night and felt the creeping dread of some unknown horror that lurks in the dark, too terrified to run or cry out because while it might be stalking silently behind you, it might be waiting for you just ahead, then you have felt a small part of what William experienced.

William's next two days flashed quickly by in a phantasmagoria of images. The demons from his past mixed companionably with those from his imagination, all bringing their messages of fear, horror and failure, depression and despair.

William felt he had been stripped bare and could have easily capitulated and accepted defeat, but his will to live and, more importantly, his sense of honor, would not let him, though at times he hated that part of himself that would not let go and surrender completely to the fear and desperation and hopelessness. Shattered in spirit, he was not broken.

There are still moments when I am attacked by echoes of that dreadful fear and I only saw it second-hand through William's mind. I see the darkness rising out of the corner of my eyes, knowing it is behind me, but when I turn and there is nothing there, cold panic still grips at my heart.

Having experienced what William saw motivating General Ryder, I know if there is a God, I have seen his opposite.

– CHAPTER 16 –

AN EARLY WARNING

HUNGER, more than the need for company, forced William to visit the mess hall for breakfast two days later. Odette, Hank and Kenji were waiting for him. Odette sprang up from their table and rushed to meet him. She hugged him, saying, "We're sorry, William," and they stood together till she gently removed her arms and led him to the table.

As he sat down, William said disconsolately, "You know, don't you, I've lost it all," and almost wept with grief. To demonstrate he bitterly punched the corner of the table and watched as drops of blood formed on one knuckle. He reflected in surprise that the physical pain came as a relief to the anguish he felt inside.

"We know," Hank said. "We felt what happened too. You are still what you have always been. Hopefully your experience has shown you there is more to what you are than you have ever considered. Remember, that is true of everyone else too and despite your resentment, temper tantrums and hurting yourself won't help either."

William became angry. He felt these people had no right to be judging him.

"You have no idea how it feels to—" Kenji cut him off before he could finish.

"You are right. We don't, so what? You're back to being a normal human again. Get over it, and fast. You won't have much time.

"The luckiest of us, maybe one in a billion, have only seen a momentary glimpse of what you have experienced for weeks. If you compare honestly who you were a year ago to who you are now, you will see you have gained a great deal. I have to leave now as our overlords have more tasks for me, but Hank knew you were going to be here now and told me to wait. We are truly your friends, William, and your kin. We would like to let you wallow in self-pity a little longer, but you don't have that luxury and we don't have the time either. The kindest thing we can do is beat you out of this mood." Kenji stood to go and to William's surprise bent to hug him strongly as he left.

Odette went with Hank to get breakfast and between them they brought back a hearty meal for William. While they were away William was forced to rapidly reassess his opinion of these people. They were not beaten, nor had they surrendered to the system that held them prisoner. More importantly, people he respected treated him as a friend and worth the effort to help. His insight was much more acute now and he could see or experience that they were not only genuine in what they said but wholeheartedly willing to help him. The realization that good still existed in the world was the spur he needed to make the Herculean effort to start to pull himself together.

As Odette and Hank put the food in front of William he thanked them.

"And not just for the food; I am more grateful for your goodwill. It has broken the spell, if you could call it that, I was under, but what do I do now?"

"We have been talking about it but can't give you an answer," Hank said. "We have no idea at this stage either. We will just have to see how the game plays out. We are lucky Argus and his stooge are away or they would know too. You have another two days, three maximum, before they return and you can be sure Argus will visit you. Be ready if you can."

Discipline and its cousin, routine, as ever, were William's saviors. After eating he walked out to the square of grass outside and began performing simple chi gong movements then continued by doing *katas*. As his body followed the familiar, ingrained patterns, his mind was captivated by the rhythm and flow and his tension slowly melted away. After a while he returned to the kitchen, screwed a handle off a broom and returned to the grass to continue with *jo katas*.

Performing the familiar drills pushed the nightmare to the back of William's mind and allowed his formidable will to take a semblance of control once more. However, this is still a work in progress. There are still times when he struggles to keep the despair and pointlessness or fear at bay.

William spent a few hours back in his room after lunch reading and finding small ways to keep himself occupied. Particularly, he watched his thoughts, determined to hunt down and weed out any that might bring a resurgence of the self-destructive part of the psyche that hides in all of us. He was determined not to fall back into that self-pitying state that seems so easy to justify by blaming it on cruel fate that has befallen us. Such self-pity is really a mask for the self-righteous self-importance that stealthily steals away our true dignity and self-respect.

When evening came he returned early to the mess and waited for the others to come. Odette was first to get there and Hank and Kenji arrived together sometime later, deep in a conversation that had obviously been going on for some time. They both greeted William warmly, then nodded to Odette before joining them at the table.

Kenji started the conversation by asking William how he was feeling so he explained to them how the meeting with General Ryder had disturbed his state of mind enough for him to lose the total peace and certainty he had experienced.

"It wasn't like being stoic or numb to the outside world; I was fully alive for the first time in my life. This increased awareness also made me deeply aware of the effect I might have on the people around me and concerned about it. I was experiencing life in a way that made my usual concerns trivial but allowed me to see and take responsibility for my own part in creating what I experienced."

Hank asked him to explain what he meant.

"I'm sorry, Hank, but I can't. If I still understood it myself, I would still be there. It is a state of mind that is not reconcilable with our usual selves. I guess the only thing that makes sense to me is to call it a state of grace—and I've lost my faith."

They left it at that and went to get their meals. As they ate, Odette asked how William's meetings with Argus had gone.

"He was not able to touch my mind at all so there was nothing he could do. Does it matter? He introduced himself to me as Wayne Jonson, by the way."

She laughed. "We know what he calls himself, but he is the most valuable asset Prometheus has so they take great pains to protect him. It's not his real name so we refuse to use it . . . Call it a meaningless gesture of defiance if you like but we enjoy playing the game. The important thing about your meetings is you have to realize it will be completely different next time. We can sense the change in your mind; it is like ours now, as vulnerable as your body. He will shuffle through it like a thief in a bank vault, not just to make sure you aren't hiding anything but to make it clear to you Prometheus owns you, body and soul. Fighting won't help. The only way is to keep your mind focused completely on the present moment, any sensations you can use to maintain your concentration—the feel of the chair you are sitting on, the tightness of your shoes—examine something you can see in minute detail or maybe watch all the sensations as you breathe in and out. You have got to keep focused; don't waver!"

Afterwards they sat outside while the evening cooled. Kenji went to his room and brought back his guitar, then played whatever he felt like. The others joined in and sang along whenever they knew the words or sometimes made some up as they went.

Hank shifted to sit by William, turned slightly toward his ear and whispered, "Only speak when Odette and Kenji are singing." When William asked why, Hank continued.

"They only keep a casual level of observation on us now but there are microphones everywhere and they still listen in from time to time. Someone may look in on us on the security cameras at any time too. What we say won't be understandable over the singing and they won't bother to record it and unscramble our conversation unless we are too obvious."

To prove his point, he stopped when Kenji changed tunes and joined in with the song for a short time before continuing quietly. "I know now Argus will be back late tomorrow evening and he will know about you immediately. You will be taken to him the morning after and we will not see you again. You will have only one chance to run, and if you want to live, you must take it. Don't hesitate."

Hank went back to joining in the songs as if nothing had happened.

William sat quietly, the dark forebodings, so recently vanquished, threatening to engulf him in terror again. But the camaraderie and simple friendliness of the evening helped William to quickly push the tsunami back.

He examined the others through the lens of his sharpened insight and could see that while on the outside they were different individuals, just fallible, self-conscious human beings, within each of them there was a core of honor and decency, goodwill and gentleness. He started his shaky steps back toward his faith in an underlying goodness behind this world, despite its apparent random, capricious insanity, that is his true strength. He silently vowed to himself never to surrender to fear again as his voice joined in with the others.

CHAPTER 17

WHEN HELP ARRIVES

WHEN THE OTHERS bade their farewells and went off to sleep, William returned to his disciplines for a few more hours before calling it a night. He slept peacefully and woke in time to go to mess, feeling rested and confident once more. Odette was already there and they ate a leisurely breakfast, though neither Hank nor Kenji appeared and remained absent for the rest of the day.

After breakfast Odette began reading a book and William sat with her. While he was relaxing he quietened his mind by feeling the state of each of his muscles, tensing them then consciously releasing the tension, working to remove any traces of the usually subconscious holding patterns of muscle stress that our bodies develop in response to our emotions. When he was satisfied, he slowed his breathing to a deep, calm and slow tempo that reinforced his physical relaxation, observing the world around him.

Calming your mind sounds easy, but in many ways it is a chimera; the effort you put into it is often just adding another layer of mental stress as results are subjective and not verifiable. Approaching your mind by relaxing your body can be much more effective. It is interesting enough to stop your mind wandering while tension in your body is a good indicator of mental stress.

It didn't take long for William's work ethic to get the better of him. So he told Odette he would catch up at lunch and left to spend a couple of hours working out as best he could with limited resources, then stretching. He kept his promise and met Odette for lunch but left soon after to practice chi gong before resting and then reading a book that had been left in his room.

Odette called on him late in the afternoon and asked him to accompany her to help set up a data projector. He followed her to stores and carried the projector after her as she carried a small speaker system to a room that opened onto the courtyard outside the mess. He cheerfully went back for an extension cord and multi-plug as she needed them to reach the projector where she wanted it put on a table toward the back of the room, facing a white-painted blank wall that had obviously been prepared after the room had been built to act as a screen.

When Odette was happy with preparations she went to the mess and left a message on the menu whiteboard that they had a new movie to watch after dinner. William knew she could have easily handled the work herself, but was including him to keep his spirits up. Rather than resenting this he was grateful for her empathy, and the company too.

Hank and Kenji arrived late again for dinner, and as Odette and William had waited for them they all ate quickly, feeling obliged to hurry as there were a few other people waiting in the mess to watch the movie, which was on the laptop Kenji had brought with him.

As the group filed in and moved toward the couches and soft seats in the middle of the room, Kenji took his laptop to the projector to set up. Hank had waited till they were last and after they walked in nudged William subtly toward some seats a few rows from the back and sat beside him. As the movie started Kenji sat on the other side of William.

William's annoyance at having to sit just in front of the sound system turned to understanding as Hank periodically gave quiet instructions to William, insisting he repeat them back and then memorize them, giving him time between each instruction.

"Make sure no one can raise the alarm as you will need some time; leave the lab through the service door at the back; turn left; go into the second room down the corridor. This is where the washing for the compound is stored. Hide there until a soldier comes to collect it. When you hear the door open, pick up a basket of washing and pretend you have just carried it in. Offer to help carry out the baskets to the soldier's truck then wait until he gets in and jump in the back and hide yourself well. The truck just goes to the laundry on another part of the base rather than outside and the routine has not changed for years so security checks are cursory at best. This is the only way we have found that will get you out of this secure compound into the rest of the base.

"Somewhere outside the laundry there will be a green Dodge Charger parked. It's unlocked; the visitor leaves his keys under the sun visor. From here you are on your own, there's nothing more we can do for you."

Hank passed William a small map of the base and asked him to destroy it after he had memorized it.

Hank refused to be drawn out or explain further. Kenji simply watched the movie and exasperated William further by saying, "You will have to trust we have done the best we can for you."

The movie ended, and Odette walked back laughing as Kenji turned the lights on.

"You ditched me. Aren't I good enough for you anymore?"

William realized immediately that Odette knew nothing about their conversation or Hank and Kenji's instructions. He also understood they trusted he was astute enough not to let on to her without them telling him.

Odette laughed as the two men stood.

"We will leave the projector until tomorrow."

Kenji joined them after disconnecting his laptop and they drifted back to the mess for a nightcap while they discussed the merits of the movie.

As they left, both Kenji and Hank bade William a friendly goodnight, but he could sense the solemn overtones of farewell, tinged with sadness, both in their words and attitude, and in himself. William could also see Odette was not aware of the seriousness of the talk as she breezily walked with him back to his room, then sauntered off into the night humming a song from the movie soundtrack.

True to Hank's prediction, William opened his door before breakfast the following morning to the stony stares of two burly MPs who had hammered loudly on his door. Taking no chances, they put him in handcuffs before asking if there was anything he wanted from the room. When he answered, "Not particularly," they escorted him away, one on each side.

He was returned to the same interview room where he had last met Argus, and after leading him over to the same chair in front of the same desk, one of the MPs made him sit while the other handcuffed each of his arms to the chair. Then they walked away to stand stolidly with their backs to the wall on either side of the door.

William was left to wait for almost an hour before Argus wandered in. He circled William and the desk once, pausing as he stood behind William. When William didn't respond or look over his shoulder, Argus finished his slow circuit, making a show of pulling out his chair and sitting.

William sat as patiently as he could, neither staring at Argus nor looking away.

"You're not invulnerable anymore, are you?"

"No."

"The unusual strength has gone too, hasn't it?" Argus continued.

"Yes."

Argus mused for a moment and William knew he was checking in his own way. He looked up finally at the MPs and said, "That will be all. Return to your posts and I will call when I want you back."

"Are you sure you'll feel safe without Tweedledum and Tweedledee to look after you?"

"I'm sure there won't be a problem, William. After all, we are both in the best possible hands—mine—but thank you for being so concerned for my welfare."

William smiled. "In that case, how about removing these handcuffs? They are uncomfortable and make it difficult for me to consider civilized conversation."

"No, William, I don't think I will. I like things just the way they are." He paused for a time then inclined his head. "Tell me about Iraq, William."

"I didn't like it, it was too hot," William answered noncommittally as his thoughts started running through his arrival and meeting with his squad. It felt like his memory was being read like a book. He couldn't stop the stream of thoughts. His struggle continued until he remembered to focus on what was happening now, filling his mind with the sensations of his breathing. Every time his mind wandered, he ruthlessly brought it back to present sensations. William was a fast learner and quickly saw that if he was intentionally trying to keep his thoughts neutral, but they kept drifting toward a particular subject, then Argus was trying to pry that information from his mind.

William realized Argus only saw what was most important or taking up most of his attention, the conscious surface levels. He focused on Argus, who he was rather than his body, and pushed back with his mind thinking strongly the words "You are a bastard."

Argus sat up in surprise, acknowledging, "Very good William, but now tell me, how are you getting on with Odette? Isn't there more than just a hint of romance in the air?"

The sudden change in direction surprised William and before he could help it, a stream of thoughts followed. William realized he actually was growing to care for her and with his typical male insensitivity in this respect (my thoughts here in case you are wondering) hadn't noticed. An echo in the back of his mind told him Argus had also noticed his affection for Odette.

William's mind jumped immediately to thoughts of Odette telling him how to prevent Argus controlling his mind. So he kicked the heel of his boot against the shin of his other leg, concentrating fiercely on the pain and using it to wipe away all other thoughts from the surface of his mind to prevent himself betraying Odette. He could sense that Argus thought he was trying to conceal his affection for Odette and had not noticed Odette's interference by assisting William.

The interrogation quickly degenerated into a contest of wills with Argus trying to pry information from William's mind while William used every strategy available to deflect the intrusions into his mind and to avoid thinking what Argus wanted to find. At one point, William projected an image of General Ryder and detected a flare of fear before it was quickly stifled. He was intrigued that Argus was afraid of the general and was distracted as he considered the implications. Argus recovered immediately, and William was once again on the defensive.

The contest ended in stalemate after more than two hours, with both men physically and emotionally exhausted. William was soaked in sweat and trembling. Argus grimaced as he stood.

"You are a capable adversary, William, but don't think this is over, or that the eventual outcome is in doubt."

He walked out the door without a backward glance. William was left for another hour before the same two MPs returned and wordlessly dragged him down the corridors to his original cell near the medical center.

– CHAPTER 18 –

THIS MUST BE THE CRISIS

THE CITY WAS BIG ENOUGH to have two large aikido dojos and several smaller ones, covering the range of styles from hard to very soft. We had visited many, most only once or twice as William said he felt it was important for me to see the differences, particularly how many thought theirs was the only "true" or "superior" style. After the third dojo in that vein, I asked William if he thought there was a genuinely superior style.

"Even if there was, it will still depend on your purpose for training in aikido. If you are doing it to increase your understanding of yourself and what you are, you will choose a different type of dojo than if you just want to learn to fight. And there are many more reasons to do aikido than that. All you can do is choose what seems best for you at the moment."

He thought for a moment then added, "I can't say any one is right but, in my humble opinion of course, any that say they are the only right or true style are almost certainly wrong. They have missed the point of aikido completely."

William had been growing more introspective over the days he had been showing me his experiences at Fort Bragg, and after a while mused, "The conscious self we experience is incredibly fleeting and fragile. We all make up our concept of who we are from the fragmentary, collected debris of our experiences, filtered through our current opinions and judgments about the world. Nobody's understanding of anything is the same. It's amazing we can communicate with each other at all, let alone agree on how to do a martial art.

"Having said that, I know from my experience there is a state beyond this where truth is absolute, not subjective or relative to experience and our arrogant opinions in any way."

On that note we left for training, which always cheered William up, followed by a relaxed dinner at a nearby restaurant. We had only stayed in the motel for two nights, then moved out to a cheap trailer park in the suburbs as William's money wasn't going to last forever. We had been there for nearly a week. This produced its own set of problems. William was very strict about not eating before training for obvious reasons, so by the time we had trained, talked and then had dinner, we were often quite late returning at night. Our erratic coming and going irritated some of the permanent inhabitants at the park, but we were quickly befriended by most.

Laura lived in a small trailer with her cat, Grief, for company. He was doing the rounds of the trailer park the morning after we arrived and noticed William sitting cross-legged in the sun after breakfast on the small deck at the trailer's door. Grief nosed around him suspiciously, but as William made no move, he climbed warily onto William's lap.

William ignored him for a while then gently stroked him and he started purring. When I opened the door, he stopped and immediately became alert and William held up his hand to stop me.

"Get me something for him if you can please."

The only thing I could find was half a cooked patty from a burger I had been too tired to finish the night before, so I took it out slowly to William on a plate. Rather than putting it down, William held it up in one hand and fed Grief little bits at a time, waiting until the cat asked for more by stretching out a paw or lifting his head toward the plate. When the patty was finished, William held the plate down in front of Grief who sniffed and licked it until he was sure there was nothing left, then stretched and sauntered off haughtily.

William bought a bag of cat biscuits while we were out that evening and waited with it for Grief next morning. A little later, an older woman who had been walking along the road in front of the row of caravans stopped to watch William feeding and playing with the cat who was sitting in his lap. The woman walked up to the deck.

"His name is Grief, if you are interested, and I'm Laura, his devoted serf," the woman said as she sat on the edge of the deck.

I was sitting in a chair at the door reading and watching William and walked out when Laura sat. William laughed, looking at the cat.

"I'm obviously bored with not enough to do, but you can call me William, if you are interested, and this is Diane," he said as I sat down too.

I burst out with the first thing that popped into my mind.

"Why on earth would you call him Grief?"

"He was a stray, abandoned in pitiful condition by someone and wild as can be when I found him," Laura said. "Tiny, too, so I called him Waif at the start but changed it to Grief because that's all he gave me, along with vet bills, at least until I had him neutered."

She winked at me then looked at William.

"I would recommend the procedure if he ever gives you trouble," she said, pointing at William.

"Thanks for the advice, I'll bear it in mind, but he appears to be behaving himself at present."

William poked out his tongue as we laughed and turned his back on both of us, disturbing Grief who hopped off his lap, walked over to butt his head on Laura's hand before curling up on her lap and purring loudly.

We chatted for some time and met regularly over the next few days. Laura introduced us to some of the other residents and obviously decided William needed mothering as she turned up with baking and advice on a regular basis. In return, William did odd jobs for her like straightening the hinge on her trailer door where it had been bent in the wind or digging over her small garden. Grief would turn up to see William arbitrarily, finding him wherever he was in the park.

Having agreed to tell me everything, William continued with his account though he was clearly distressed by the memories at this stage of his life. He was left in his cell for three days. An orderly arrived three times a day with meals, accompanied by an armed guard, neither of whom uttered a word. On the morning of the fourth day the two MPs arrived, handcuffs at the ready, to move William. To his surprise they just shifted him down the corridor to the lab where Brian, Alan, Argus and, more surprisingly, Odette were waiting.

Brian nodded toward the shiny, new examination table with lots of extra restraints and the MPs frog-marched William over to it. William felt a small sense of satisfaction as he remembered why the table had needed to be replaced. He took off his shirt and lay on it when ordered, not wanting to give up his dignity by being forced to and submitted gracefully when Odette was ordered to strap him down. When the straps had been checked, the handcuffs were removed and the MPs ordered to leave.

Argus walked over to stare down at William.

"I have been in touch with the general. He is still indisposed and so can't be here today, but he seems very angry about what you did to him, William."

William protested that he had not done anything to General Ryder.

"He does not see it that way," Argus said. "He seems to think his mind is not quite his own anymore, or something like that. There are new thoughts there he does not want to think, and he feels that makes him weak."

Argus bent down and whispered in William's ear.

"Psychopaths don't accept doubt about their God-given right to do whatever they want, or about their own infallibility as well, particularly in their own mind.

"Regardless of the problem, he definitely blames you and enthusiastically ordered we try testing you to destruction to see if that defense mechanism in your mind kicks in again."

"It won't," William said.

"No matter, it will be interesting to see what happens either way," Argus said.

I interrupted William's flow of thoughts at this point, asking "Why won't it work? Surely that is why your mind did whatever it did—to protect you."

William pulled himself back to the present moment to answer my question and shook his head sadly.

"If it was that easy, I could make it happen again too," he said ruefully.

"A mind that needs to defend itself is automatically saying it is not invulnerable. Defense and attack are both equally unthinkable in that state. A mind that cannot be harmed cannot harm another because the thought of harm does not exist. If it thought it could do harm, it would also know it could be harmed."

William returned to his earlier train of thought. Argus was saying, "We needed to come up with something that will kill you slowly, forcing your mind to defend yourself. It took a little ingenuity, but the good doctor has come up with a clever concoction that fits all the requirements nicely." He gestured in the direction of one of the lab benches at a small beaker of clear liquid. "That will eat right through you if you don't stop it."

He turned to Odette and snapped out an order.

"Bring it here."

She walked over to the bench and picked up the beaker, being careful to pull on a rubber glove first.

"You mustn't do this; it is wrong," she said.

"Are you defying a direct order from a superior officer?" Argus said. "Bring it here!"

Odette quailed under his verbal and emotional assault, walking toward him with the beaker trembling slightly in her hand. Argus had all his concentration focused on her and William knew he was forcing her to obey. He was aware of the others in the room and could see they obtained some sort of perverse enjoyment from making Odette participate in William's torment, her subjection to their positions of power. A hierarchy based on bullying needs victims to survive. While someone else was the victim, they were safe.

Odette reached Argus as her struggle climaxed. She gritted her teeth.

"I will not let you do this," she said, throwing the beaker onto the floor where the spilled liquid started foaming slightly. An acrid smell filled the air. Brian ran to the bench and pulled a quart bottle from the cupboard underneath it, walked over and poured some of the liquid on the spill. It stopped foaming.

"Stupid girl; this makes no difference at all," Argus said. "There is a whole bottle still under the bench and Doctor Key can make up more from the reagents in the room in a couple of minutes if you destroy that too."

He turned to the other men and snapped, "Restrain her," expecting immediate acquiescence. Instead they stared nervously at Odette as she glared back at them with both hands clenched, daring them to try.

William and Argus both recognized the nature of the problem immediately. Both of the other men, the doctor and the psychologist, were career professionals, academics at best, while Odette, as a nurse at field hospitals, was a well-trained soldier. Acting together, they could most likely overpower her, but they were not willing to take the risk or accept the damage they would certainly incur in the process.

Argus sighed derisively and moved to deal with the situation himself, but the whole tableau froze as William said quietly, "Stop." Argus turned to William, but William was focused on Odette as he said, "Odette, promise me you won't interfere."

"William, I can't," she said as a tear started to form in the corner of her eye. She did not turn to him but kept her eyes on the other men.

No one moved as William waited patiently then repeated the words, exactly as before. He waited again as she shook with emotion, refusing to weep in front of these people she detested, then said finally with nothing but kindness in his voice, "Promise me."

She turned to look William in the eye and, without a trace of subservience, said, "William, I promise you I will do nothing to interfere," then added with steel in her voice, "but I will do nothing to help them either."

William turned to Argus. "Does that satisfy you?"

Argus paused while he measured Odette up for a moment before replying coolly, "For the moment," his tone promising there would be retribution later.

He carried a lab stool to the empty wall near the door, out of harm's way, and ordered Odette to sit there, which she did meekly. Then he told the doctor to get the pistol he kept for his personal safety.

"How do you know about the gun?" Brian asked.

Argus cut him off by gazing heavenward.

"God help me . . . Just get it, damn you."

Brian walked stiffly over to the bench, fishing a key out of his pocket as he went. He unlocked a drawer under the bench, pulling it open to lift out a small P-90 pistol. The pathos of the situation: Brian needing a pistol to feel secure in the face of his victims, but keeping it locked away for fear one of them might get it themselves and use it on him ensured the gesture was futile—if a situation arose where he did need it, there was little chance he would get to it in time—made William feel sad for him despite the fear he was feeling for himself.

Brian hesitantly brought the pistol to Argus, who clicked off the safety and placed it gently against William's temple but looked at Odette.

"If you so much as move, I will kill him before I shoot you, understand?"

Odette nodded mutely so Argus put the gun in his shirt pocket, leaving the safety off.

He turned to Brian.

"Get some more."

Brian returned to the bench, lifted out a large canister, opened a draw to get out another small beaker and, after nearly filling it, delivered it to Argus who without ceremony poured it on William's chest.

William let out a small gasp, more from shock at the situation than from the initial pain. Within seconds, however, the pain had blossomed into agony. Argus struck at William's mind as the pain racked him. William could sense his lust to find the secret of invulnerability that he was sure lay hidden somewhere in the recesses of William's mind.

William tried to show Argus that his intense desire for personal safety and power made it impossible for him to ever achieve it. Argus was not able to believe him; it did not make any sense from his view of the world.

In desperation, William hurled all he had seen and learned from General Ryder's mind at Argus who simply thought back with an overtone of desolation and intense sadness.

"I know, what does that change for me—or you?" and continued his relentless attack.

When William knew he could last no more, rather than surrender, with his last resources he spread his senses deeper into his body, both creating and sensing a firm impression of his heart and all the mechanisms that controlled it, right back to his brain.

"Stop," he commanded.

Hearing Argus screaming, "No, don't," both with his ears and in his mind, William died.

CHAPTER 19

REBIRTH

THE SHOCK OF SHARING those experiences was devastating. I fainted. William put me to bed.

When I woke late the next morning, William was sitting by the bed in the trailer. I lay quietly, glaring at him. William was impassive, and I was angry.

"You died?"

"Yes," he answered.

"I felt you die."

"Yes."

"But you're alive."

I got a slow single nod along with the "Yes" this time—what an improvement. "Tell me why, how," I pleaded.

"As soon as you want, we can continue."

"No! I just want you to tell me," I was adamant. "I don't want to live through stuff like that ever again."

"Why not?" he said. "After all, you have insisted—against my better judgment too, I might add—that I relive it all so you could understand. To be honest, I don't know why the mental link between you and me has grown the way it has, why you have been able to see or experience my memories, but now I believe it is really important, too. I have been thinking it over and it may just be another arrogant delusion on my part, but I will wait until you are ready to continue. I have to trust the process."

Some of it didn't make sense to me, so while I could not face looking at William's memories I asked him to explain what I had seen, plying him with questions. Mostly he said when I had seen more, it should explain things. The only interesting question William would answer was why had Argus bothered with Odette at all? He had the two MPs who had brought William in—they would have happily strapped William down and left when ordered, no problem. Odette, on the other hand, was definitely a complication. She didn't need to be there at all.

"His reasons were much more complex than you think," William said thoughtfully. "Argus knew having Odette there would affect me because he now knew I liked her and he wanted to use her to shame or humiliate me. If I was feeling embarrassed and angry at being helpless in front of her while he was all-powerful it would put me off balance, weaken my mental focus as I wouldn't be thinking just about how to resist him, making it easier for him to take control of my mind.

"Secondly, forcing Odette to strap me in and bring him the beaker, even though she desperately did not want to, was an explicit threat. He was demonstrating his power over her with the implication she would suffer more if I didn't cooperate. This part backfired on him as he pushed her a little further than he should have and she broke free of the psychological hold, obedience despite her personal feelings, he had been establishing.

"I think, though, what was more important to Argus was Odette herself as he was sure what he had planned for me would break my resistance— and he was right. For a long time, Odette had been forced to help with the lab experimentation even though it was contrary to her nature. If he had forced Odette to take part in something she really hated, something that was an atrocity to her, he would have taken a big step in turning her into one of his pawns. I keep seeing people in power who are cruel, cynical manipulators while friends who knew them tell me they were starry eyed idealists when they were young. We lose our humanity or honor or whatever we value about ourselves in small pieces, but each step down that path makes it harder to return.

"Hank, Kenji and Odette, along with others like them I'm sure, were a thorn in Argus's side. They seemingly did as they were ordered but had never truly capitulated, so I suspect he had hoped to push Odette into abandoning her principles in the knowledge it would be much easier for him to achieve next time. He had been working on turning Odette into a weapon against the others."

William fell silent, consumed by his memories as he sat beside me on the bed.

"One other thing while I think of it," he continued. "Can you understand now why I so overreacted and walked out on you when I thought you were snooping around in my head? The specter of those events still haunts me. I know I have said I was sorry, but I still feel guilty and embarrassed for letting you down."

I reached over to take his hand and pull him into a hug, neither of us needing to say a word, then he went out leaving me to sleep a little longer.

William brought me breakfast with a cup of tea then disappeared until lunchtime when he came in with a sandwich, apple doughnut and a large paper cup full of coffee—a peace offering, I presumed.

"Changed your mind yet?" I asked hopefully.

He just smiled smugly.

"What do you think?"

I thought, *Sandpaper couldn't wear him down during an entire geological era*, but couldn't be bothered saying it. We went for a short run later and as I was feeling better went to training in the evening.

Even though I was tired I slept fitfully during the night, knowing William would never relent now and finish his story verbally. I could also see I was in danger of running away. I was back in the grip of the fear, that nameless dread that had flooded William after his confrontation with General Ryder. I knew if I didn't continue soon I never would and if I didn't I would eventually be beaten by the fear.

After we had worked through our usual exercises the next morning, then had breakfast, I said to William, "I surrender, let's get on with it." There was not the slightest flicker of emotion across his face to show if he was surprised by this or had been expecting it. He walked around the table to sit opposite me and after staring at me for a time, establishing the link, he spoke some words I could not understand as my consciousness seemed to fade.

The identification was much stronger this time than it had ever been before. I felt hands on my (William's) chest and a voice saying, almost begging:

"You've got to live, damn you."

There was a sudden feeling of wholeness and I felt my heart start beating, the familiar sound or feeling was comforting. I hadn't realized until then it was missing. Taking a first shuddering breath, I opened my eyes to bright light shining in them and wanted to close them, but knew I shouldn't.

My arm moved. It was free. I knew this was important but couldn't think why. There was a girl standing over me, hands still on my chest. Tears rolled down her cheeks when she saw me move. She disappeared to come back and start drying me with a towel, someone must have poured water all over me. I thought *this should be hurting*, and put my hand to my chest, confused because I remembered the skin burning, but it seemed fine.

I tried to sit up and she put her hands on my chest to stop me.

I slurred, "Have to."

I tried again. She relented and swung my legs off the table to counterbalance my effort to sit up. With her help, I managed to sit on the edge of the table with my feet on the floor. I felt her as she dried my back then put a shirt on me, buttoning it up for me as my fingers had fumbled and I couldn't remember how. Odette saw my hat and handed it to me. I held it numbly in my hand.

Sitting up had let me see the floor. There were two men crouched around another who was unconscious on the floor. One had a box with wires attached to paddles he was holding in his hand. It didn't mean anything to me. A thought flashed through my head.

It's a defibrillator, dummy, and with a wrench I was back in my own head or at least aware of my own mind as I watched the stream of William's memories. There was a break as he clearly thought, *Who are you calling a dummy?*, before normal programming resumed.

William was in shock, but his memory was returning. He noticed the pistol was now in Odette's pocket and realized she was currently in control of the situation. When he could stand he walked with her help to the back of the lab and saw the door Hank had mentioned.

"I know what I have to do. I have to go." He hugged her and continued. "I need time, give me as much as you can."

"I will, William," she said.

She kissed him lightly as she turned away. She walked over to the chair Argus had placed against the wall and sat down. She took the gun carefully from her pocket. "If any one of you makes any sound or any move I don't approve of, I will shoot you all," she said conversationally.

William stepped into the corridor knowing he had all the time he would need.

It was a good thing the instructions had been simple. Turn left, go in the second door, hide. Even in William's state it wasn't that difficult. He saw the baskets and sacks of washing thrown in a jumbled pile and wormed his way in. The laundry truck was late so he had to wait nearly an hour before it arrived. The break was enough for William to be functioning almost normally, regardless of how he felt. He heard the truck arrive and cracked the door to look back in the corridor. There was no one there so he grabbed a laundry sack and stepped into the corridor. When he heard the door open to the outside he counted to ten then stepped back into the room with the sack. A corporal was carrying out the first basket and William offered to help him. If he thought there was anything odd in a lieutenant carrying a laundry bag or offering to help him with a manual task, he had the wisdom not to mention it.

As William threw the last sack into the truck, he said, "I'll shut the door."

He walked into the building and watched the corporal walk to the cab of his truck, slipped back out and shut the door. He climbed into the open back of the truck and once again hid in a pile of laundry. The truck drove to the gate leading out of the compound into the main base and stopped. William held his breath while the guards had a quick look in the back of the truck but didn't even bother checking the pile of sacks.

William had a good sense of direction and was alarmed when he realized the truck hadn't turned toward the laundry when it left the compound. Hank hadn't mentioned this. He looked cautiously out the back but before he could decide what to do the truck stopped outside another building and he was forced to hide once more. More laundry was thrown in and he realized the truck was still doing its rounds. It started off once more and William compared its route with the base map he had memorized, deciding there were a barracks and an administration block between him and the laundry. He hoped the truck would stop at both and decided he would get out at the last stop as it was closest to his destination.

When he stopped at the barracks he noticed the corporal took a long time to get his sack and bring it back to the truck. He changed his mind in a flash, seeing this might be his best chance, and as the corporal walked back into the building, glanced out the back and stepped down onto the road. There were other soldiers around, but no one thought anything out of the ordinary in a soldier stepping out of an Army truck. He knew, though, that if the corporal recognized him outside the compound, it would be all over, so he strode off smartly while trying not to be obvious in his haste, refusing to look back.

No one took a second look at him as he walked past the admin block toward the laundry. He couldn't see the car and was starting to worry as it was not in the car parks along the front of the building. Not knowing what to do, he kept walking past the building and saw the car parked at the far end of the loading dock at the back and turned to walk toward it.

His anxiety mounted the closer he got to the car. Through the open doors he walked past he could see the occasional soldier in uniform mixed in with civilian workers. He opened the door, sat behind the wheel and reached up, finding the keys behind the visor as promised. He paused as the enormity of his actions caught up with him. If he left the base he was a deserter, and he was loyal by nature. It may not seem like a big step, but it was still a chasm for him to cross. He would burn his bridges with all that his life had been; all his hopes, plans and ambitions, everything he had worked so hard for, would turn to dust if he stepped into that unknowable future.

An image of Odette sitting strangely proud and at peace crossed his mind. William fiercely turned the key, grimly determined.

He drove slowly away from the loading dock, expecting to hear alarms or yells or any sort of response. The silence was almost as unnerving as discovery would have been. He knew where to find the gate and drove toward it, pulling his hat down to cover his face. He slowed as he approached the barrier, not knowing what else to do while his mind feverishly tried to come up with clever diversions. None of it mattered. The car and its usual driver were well known. The barrier lifted and he was waved through. If the guard had any second thoughts or noticed anything amiss he didn't respond. William was free.

CHAPTER 20

THINGS ARE GOING WELL . . .

"THAT WAS INTERESTING," William said. "At first you didn't seem to be there at all, then you're back and yelling insults at me."

"Interesting!" I spluttered. "I was you. I thought and experienced everything you did. I didn't remember me at all. Seeing your memories is one thing but this—" I faltered.

William nodded. "I see your point. It doesn't seem to have done you any harm though. In fact, I am sure being me can only have been an enlightening and heartwarming experience. Count yourself blessed. Only you out of the countless millions who applied have been so specially favored."

"Someone help," I begged. "I have been infected by terminal smugness and conceit. It starts out as a minor sense of superiority and ends with delusions of being god. There is no cure."

William smiled. "What's the problem? When you are perfect, why would you need a cure?"

"When you thought of Odette as you got in the car you felt guilty . . . You still do now, don't you? Why?"

He sighed. "She openly helped me, and I left her to whatever vengeance Argus would exact. He was already angry enough at her disobedience. I didn't have to involve her; it was just what was easiest for me. There are other ways I could have handled it. If I had tied them all up, Odette included, I could still have got away without the blame falling on her."

"You can't know that," I replied. "Argus would probably have died if the others hadn't been allowed to revive him; he looked sick enough and you wouldn't want that on your conscience. You weren't strong enough at that stage either. Besides, I am sure she felt guilty for all she had been forced to do in the lab. When she first stood up to Argus, it made no difference, she was easily brushed aside. But later, when she helped you escape, it made a difference. She was able to atone in some way, redeem herself in her own eyes. I saw her too and when she sat back on that stool she was proud. She was saying to Argus you put me here, helpless, and I still have won. She has found her honor again. Don't you dare take that from her by feeling sorry or guilty."

Tears filmed in his eyes, but he said nothing. *Can't bear the idea of someone sacrificing themselves for him*, I thought, serious self-worth issues hidden there somewhere.

"Okay then, how about Hank and Kenji? Couldn't they have made it all a lot easier for Odette? She didn't have to be kept in the dark, did she? Why not blame them instead of yourself?" I asked.

"They couldn't have handled it any differently," William smiled. "In fact, they surprised me with what they were able to do. Between the two of them they managed to foretell very accurately what was going to happen, and at the same time see enough around the base to give me an almost foolproof escape route. All they gave me was a set of instructions. It wasn't even clear I would get the chance. There is a momentum in the present that tells us what the future should be, but I am sure we still shape the future by our present choices. Their instructions were so nebulous I had little idea when or if I would use them. If they had told me, 'you will have to escape during your second meeting with Argus,' I would have consciously had to conceal that from Argus and that attempt would have drawn his attention because of the focus of my attention.

"Then there's Odette. She had to make her own choices—freely. If she were told 'It all depends on you. You have to openly defy Argus, then bring William back when he's dead,' do you really think she could have done it? Talk about performance anxiety. Not to mention Argus would sense her unusual anxiety and know something was wrong. There is no way they could have prepared her without changing what happened. They did exactly what they had to do, no more no less. I can't fault them."

"If you won't listen to me, listen to what you just said and accept none of it is your fault either," I said. "Stop taking it all so seriously. Holding on to guilt, justified or not, is often just another kind of egotism. Self-pity is the same. Attitudes people use to make themselves feel important. You don't need it. It's time to let it go, regrets and all, and move on. You keep telling me to live fully in the present. How 'bout you man up and do the same? Take a dose of your own medicine."

He looked at me sheepishly for a while before shrugging as he took a deep breath and breaking into a rueful smile.

"Okay, you've got me on that one. It always amazes me how clearly I sometimes see where other people are off balance, physically or mentally, and don't see it in myself. I will deal with it."

It felt to me as if a burden was falling from his shoulders, that he was lighter in spirit. It takes a huge effort of will to change a mindset and I could see or more correctly could sense he had committed himself to making that effort. Not that any change like that happens automatically or easily. "I *will* hold you to that," I stated flatly. He knew I meant it.

That was enough for both of us. We drove into the downtown area for the rest of the day. It was a change from hanging out at the trailer park or walking in parks. When I got tired of looking in the shops and ignoring William's displeasure at having to go shopping I went to an information center and asked about local landmarks with interesting history. We both enjoyed the afternoon and learned lots. Every city has a tale or two to tell.

Aikido that evening was interesting. The number of people training was unusually small and most there were advanced, or Dan grades, so later in the session the sensei started showing some counters to the techniques he had started the class with. He made sure everyone practiced them slowly and smoothly.

"It is really important to get the form and the feel right first, then you can speed it up later," the sensei said. "If you start off with bad form then each time you practice it, it gets harder to eradicate. Being able to do your techniques very fast but badly is still just doing them badly." He emphasized that any tendency to struggle or fight something that wasn't working well increased tension and resistance, both in yourself and in your partner.

"I show you counters because they teach you where the natural holes in your technique are, not to justify or increase your competitiveness."

William and I were a picture of contrast as we went off to get dinner. He had had a great time seeing some new things and being able to work on them with other capable practitioners, he was feeling ebullient. On the other hand, I found the second half of the class extremely frustrating. I was still not that confident with my basic movements let alone able to change techniques used on me. It all adds up to developing your sensitivity to opportunities that each moment presented and being able to exploit them effectively. I was clearly not there yet and consequently felt annoyed and resentful.

William noticed my lack of enthusiasm, and asked what was up so I made some snarky comment about feeling inadequate in the face of all that competence.

"Would you call a baby inadequate that had not yet learned to walk or Nureyev inadequate before he learned ballet?" he said. "We can only be inadequate if we judge ourselves and our actions by some external, artificial standard. That can only lead to guilt or self-pity as you so kindly pointed out to me this morning," he thoughtfully reminded me with a smug look on his face.

Oh God, hoisted on my own petard. No one should be expected to live up to their own good advice—unless it's William of course. It's just not natural. However, I could appreciate the irony of the situation. We shared a happy, lighthearted evening after that.

We were in no hurry to return to the trailer and sat together on a couch at the restaurant, looking out at the city from the second floor. I was leaning contentedly against William's shoulder and turned my cell phone on to see if there were any messages from my family back home. I hadn't checked for a couple of days and was surprised to see two messages from a local number I didn't recognize. Chills ran down my spine as I opened the first and read it. It was from Laura. I sat up and handed the phone to William saying, "You'd better read this."

Hi Dearie, two men came by in a car after lunch. They were showing a picture of William in an army uniform and asked me and some of the others here if we had seen him. They know he has been staying here. It seems odd so let him know please.

William's happy mood evaporated as he read, and he grimly opened the next text. I read it over his shoulder.

Late afternoon, two more men brought the manager over. They looked in your trailer. GOOD LUCK.

"Just when things were looking up," William said. He slumped down into the couch dejectedly.

"Why now?" I asked.

"We have been talking about Argus, thinking about him, hating him probably, for days. He will have sensed it," William said. "We may as well have set up a huge neon sign saying here we are. I should have been prepared, it's so obvious."

"Isn't this where we leap into action?" I insisted. The anxiety building from sitting there doing nothing was quickly getting to me. "If they are that close to us, shouldn't we be leaving now or something?"

"Leaping into action without knowing what we are leaping into is probably the dumbest thing we could do right now," he said.

"Well forgive my metaphor. It should be obvious I meant leap away from the action, in any direction, as far and as fast as possible."

"That is not what I meant. I am trying to think of the implications before I do anything rash. If they have been in the trailer they won't have found anything with my name on it, but there are a number of things with your name on it, your passport and airline tickets among them. If nothing else, we need to get them so you can leave. They won't have taken them yet as they won't be sure, but they will know who you are now and will soon have pictures of you."

My heart sank further as I realized there was a lot more to this than I first thought.

"But I don't have to leave," I countered. "I won't leave. I am going to stay with you whether you like it or not. Don't you dare try and get rid of me."

"That's not the issue. If you stay here with me, you become an overstayer and lose your legal rights. If they catch me, you will be left with nothing. Actually, nothing would be far better than what they will do to you because you know about me. Forget all those romantic notions of running away together, you and me against the world and all that crap. That only works if the world doesn't give a damn. It cannot work with what is arrayed against us. I will not argue with you, but I promise you I will not abandon you when you leave. If you try and stay, I *will*. I will not destroy your life. Believe it or not, that is because I truly do care."

He slumped back into a broody silence.

"I feel a decided lack of inspiration; my muse must be musing somewhere else. Let's go," William said as he stood up.

We went up to the counter and William asked if they could tell him somewhere he could use the Internet in the middle of the night. They sent him to an all-night video store that had a few computers a couple of blocks away.

We drove there, and I went in with William. He searched maps of the suburbs around the trailer park and maps of the city with the roads leading out, printing copies of the ones he was interested in. He also searched long-haul trucking companies that worked out of the central city. I asked why.

"It's something I haven't tried before. It may be a way of getting out of here."

We drove in the direction of the trailer park.

"What we need is a distraction," William said, "something to lure them all away. Unfortunately, that's us. I am pretty sure they will be expecting you to be with me, so if you are not, one of them will probably stay behind in case you turn up. Whether you like it or not, you are along for the ride . . .

"I've got it," William exclaimed as he swung the car around, driving to the 7-Eleven we got our groceries from. He ran in, leaving me in the car, and came back with a large paper bag. In it were short flat head nails, tacks and a few glass jars along with some other things. He spent five minutes in the car park showing me how to make caltrops with what he had bought.

While I slowly made and filled the glass jars with caltrops, William circled the streets away from the trailer park, getting a feel of possible places that he could drive to. He found what he wanted—a long, narrow suburban street that was open at both ends where using the caltrops would be easy—and decided he was ready.

"Right," he grinned at me, "now we can leap into action."

– CHAPTER 21 –

CHANGING PLANS

AS WE HEADED BACK to the trailer park William said, "When we are almost at the park, I want you to call Laura, ask her to say the name of the cat if she feels safe to talk. If she says yes and she is happy to help us, then ask her to come to her door. When she sees us pull up in the car ask if she will run out and shout as if she is warning us off. That's it. If she can't do that then we will have to come up with another plan quickly."

"What plan?" I asked, "And why do you keep saying we? I don't recall discussing anything."

"No," he answered, "but you are included in the plan so that makes it alright."

"Sure it does," I muttered. "So why are you involving Laura, after all we were talking about this morning?"

"The agents will be expecting us to go to our trailer and are unlikely to close in on us until we get out of the car and go in. We are much harder to stop if we are still in the car. If we go down the lane to our trailer they can block us in by parking a car across the lane. If we get that far we are finished so most likely they will wait a bit.

"Laura's trailer is on the main avenue that loops back to the entrance. I want it to look like it is just a social call on Laura as we drive in and that she warns us so we flee. It's strategy. From their point of view, we don't know they are waiting for us and their cars will be reasonably well hidden. If I just drive around the loop and out again they would most likely guess I already knew they were there. Then they would wonder why I would take the risk and someone bright might decide I'm actually trying to lead them away. I don't want to make it easy for them to reach that conclusion, so Laura is the only way I can think of that someone might warn us. If you would like to give me a couple of days, I will come up with something better. All this double-think makes my head hurt but it's the only way I stay alive."

We were almost there.

"You need to make the call now."

I did, and Laura surprised me by agreeing without hesitation. William sped up and within a minute he turned in the entrance, driving slowly toward our trailer. He pulled up outside Laura's place and rather than waiting, stepped out the door and sauntered up the short path to the door. As he lifted his hand to knock, Laura burst out looking flustered and started talking wildly.

William turned on his heel, loped to the car and jumped in. True to his prediction a car had pulled in to the entrance while we were stopped outside Laura's. If we had driven straight to our trailer, we would not have seen it. It pulled over as the driver saw our car pulled up to one side of the avenue.

The car behind made no move until we passed the lane to our trailer, then started off in pursuit. William had a good lead by this stage but as we rounded the last bend and could see the entrance, a second car raced off the street and slewed sideways, blocking the entrance.

We're done for, I thought.

"Good, that's both of them," William said. He braked hard, looking like he was going to stop but as he screeched toward the car, he veered to the side, jumping the low curb with a crash before sliding over the carefully manicured lawn and smashing down the eight-foot cypress that was one of a pair framing the entrance. After hurtling over the footpath, we reached the road and William roared off, revving the engine to redline as he worked his way up through the gears. I would like to say we left them in our dust, but it wasn't like that. William had brought the car because it was old, cheap and unmemorable.

The car following us didn't chance William's impromptu exit and had to wait for the other car blocking the entrance to back up. But even with that lead, we didn't have a hope of escaping. The first car caught up with us when we were only halfway to William's chosen street, but the occupants were content to cruise behind us, waiting for their partners to catch up.

William, though busy doing his best to make a challenge of the mismatched contest, had been nervously darting glances in his rear-vision mirror.

"Here comes the cavalry," he said as a second set of lights streaked up from behind. The driver swung into the left lane, intent on getting in front of us to cut us off. He hit the brakes, slewing slightly sideways as William swerved across the center line to block him off. The car that had been behind us accelerated to try and pass us on the inside and William swerved back to block him. William managed to hold them back a second time.

"This is not going to work, we will have to deal with them now. Get ready with the caltrops. Throw one bottle on each side of the road when I tell you," he said as he opened his window. I opened mine as well.

As he pulled back into the right lane to block the first car but overdid it slightly, leaving space for the other car to try to pass, it surged forward for the third time. William swung left as if he was trying to block them again and actually bounced off the side of their car back into the right lane as they pulled past us. He timed it perfectly. As the car pulled into the right lane in front of us to block us in between it and the other car behind us and it hit the brakes, William spun the steering wheel to the left and pulled on the handbrake, spinning across the road into the other lane, facing back the way we had been coming from. The car that had been following us was not so quick and hit the other car nose to tail, adding to the confusion.

I started to throw a jar out my window.

"Wait," William said. "When we are going faster they will spread better. When you do, throw them up so we are well past before they spread."

In another couple of seconds, he said, "Now!" I leaned out the window to throw one back, high over the trunk on my side. The jar smashed and the contents spread beautifully. I whipped back as fast as I could to throw one out William's window to cover the other lane as well, narrowly missing his nose. He glared at me, so I shrugged my shoulders at him in a 'what can you expect under the circumstances' kind of way.

I reached for the other two jars. "Don't throw them yet until we know we need them," he said. "I hadn't wanted to use them on a major road because of the mayhem it will cause. We shouldn't compound the damage if we can avoid it."

He had screeched to the right down another wide street and was racing as fast as he could. When our pursuers turned onto the street we were on, they barreled after us with renewed intensity, catching us despite the distance we had put between us. William strung it out as long as he could, but they caught up.

"They haven't noticed yet, but their tires should be going soft by now. Let's see how they handle hard braking and cornering at the same time."

William hit the brakes and veered left into another street, our tires squealing their outrage at this mistreatment and the car leaning alarmingly on the suspension. The others were going much faster in their effort to overtake us, but they had no chance. The back wheels of the lead car broke loose and it slid sideways into the traffic light pole on the corner, while the second car under-steered straight into the near side of the first car.

I let out a cheer and William slowed a little but drove on back to the trailer park swiftly.

"Don't celebrate too soon," he cautioned, "they may still be able to get backup. We are not out of the woods yet."

As we drove back in the entrance, our headlights showed two deep furrows in the lawn where our car had hurtled over it and the smashed tree.

"Warwick's going to be really pissed off when he sees that in the morning," I opined.

"You focus on getting your gear in the car, I will look after mine, whoever finishes first helps the other."

We drove as quietly as possible up to our trailer. He jumped out and opened the trunk before running inside, his sense of urgency spurring me on too. He grabbed his pack in one hand and a bag from the bathroom and had thrown them in the trunk before I had my spare clothes off their hangers and lined up on the bed. William swept them up in one armful and grabbed my open pack with the other hand.

"Anything you can get as you follow me, bring. Otherwise leave it."

I rushed after him, grabbing what I could and followed him to the car, leaving some of my books and other cherished mementos behind. I understood now why he never unpacked anything unless he was using or wearing it and always put it back when he was finished with it. Surprisingly, abandoning a few meaningless trinkets hurt more than makes sense in the extremity of the situation. It seemed to tap some unknown well of loss and loneliness in me. As we drove off into the night once more to God knows where, I choked back a sob.

William completely misunderstood what I was feeling.

"Don't be afraid, we've got away with it. We should be safe now."

"I'm not afraid."

William and I were both surprised by my vehemence and lapsed into an awkward silence. William had enough to think about anyway. We heard sirens in the distance, so he dropped off the main street, heading for suburban streets where we were less likely to be seen, not knowing if they were looking for us or not.

I cooled down very quickly. Being angry at each other could only be counterproductive, if not terminal.

"William, I'm sorry if I hurt your feelings, I didn't mean to snap at you."

"That's okay," he replied. "I understand now."

I looked at him and could see he actually did understand. At his best, his uncanny sense of connection or empathy meant he often felt what others around him were feeling, even me most of the time.

He pulled over into a gas station, parking on the edge of the forecourt so the attendant couldn't see the dented side of the car and asked if there was somewhere cheap nearby we could stay the night. The attendant pointed us in the direction of a youth hotel a couple of blocks away. William wanted to get the car out of sight as soon as possible and assumed they would have off street parking.

He walked around to the trunk and started rummaging around in his pack, finally pulling out a little device a bit smaller than a cell phone.

"I bought this in one of my more paranoid moments. It's an RF detector that checks for radio output. It's never been any use to me up to now, but I have a strong feeling I should check."

He started moving it around our packs, moving from one to the other and turning them over from time to time.

"Ah, there it goes," he said happily, as a light flashed while he had the detector over his pack. "It's nice to know my intuition still does work occasionally. We just had to wait for it to send a position report."

It took William some time to find the bug in his pack as it was a shiny metal box only a little longer than a car key. He dropped it on the concrete and smashed it under his heel, then shifted my pack to the back seat. He gave me the detector.

"Keep checking while I drive, there may be one in your pack too, but I don't think so."

William was driving at a sedate pace.

"You said before something about your intuition still working. What did you mean?" I asked.

"Usually I just know things, like when they are closing in on me again and it's time to move on. They haven't got this close to me since just after I escaped, but since I met you, I, or should I say we, have been lucky to get away several times."

"Well don't blame me," I said. "I'm just here for the scenery and the scintillating conversation."

He glared at me over his shoulder.

"I'm not blaming you. My mind needs to be calm, serene maybe, for my intuition to work reliably because that way I notice the tiny changes to my peace of mind that say something is wrong or the little nudges from my unconscious mind that tell me to do something. They may not always make any rational sense to me at the time I feel them, but I have learned to trust those gentle directives and they have never put me wrong. At present my head is full of reliving old wounds and probably all tangled up with some new emotions, too. All that mental noise makes hearing the whisperings of my subconscious unlikely."

He paused a moment as we drove into the hotel driveway, then after we parked reached back to take my hand and finished with a smile.

"So when I think about it, maybe I should be blaming you after all."

CHAPTER 22

PRICE OF FREEDOM

WILLIAM PAID FOR A ROOM for two nights and asked the receptionist if we could leave the car in the lot for a couple of days while attending a revivalist seminar nearby. We went back out to the car and put everything we could into our packs while William scrawled a note and left it with the pink slip for the car in the glove box.

We dropped our packs off in the room and I lay on the bed while William slipped out to use the phone. I collapsed into a deep sleep and didn't hear him return, so the next thing I knew he was shaking my shoulders.

"Wake up, we need to go now. I've left it as long as I can."

He already had a pack in each hand as I groggily stood up and he handed me mine. He checked there was no one in the corridor before stepping out and threw the room key onto the bed. As we walked away from the stairs to reception William smiled at me.

"Your tour company has arranged another novel experience to help ensure this vacation is going to be one you will always treasure."

He stopped at the door to the fire escape at the end of the corridor and opened it with a flourish.

"Unfortunately, not after you." He stepped out. "Close the door quietly, and I did check, it's not alarmed."

There was a tiny landing, but the stairs, more like a ladder, were so narrow and steep he had to turn and back down, holding on carefully to stop his pack overbalancing him. He had to take care, but for me it was a nightmare.

While I am used to carrying a heavy pack, backing down two stories of ladders with it threatening to overbalance me with every backward step was terrifying. It's something I never want to do again. Ever true to his word, William was again providing me with another night to remember.

We started walking as soon as I was on the ground and William apologized.

"We couldn't go out past the receptionist with our full packs, at this time of night. If he suspected we were ditching the car, he would most likely call the police and they would be here in minutes as I am sure they will have been alerted to look out for it. As it stands, the hotel people probably won't check up on it for three or four days by which time we will be well gone.

"As to why we have to get out right now, obviously we can't keep using the car, and as a pair we are too noticeable to use the bus, so I phoned around some of the trucking companies who shift freight twenty-four hours a day to see if we could bum a ride out west. It was a long shot, and generally they laughed at me and hung up, but one guy passed me on to the depot foreman. Their nightshift is down a couple of men, due to a party or something, and they have a couple of rigs that need to be loaded by this morning. They will give us a ride out to Seattle in the morning if I work what's left of the shift, so we need to get there fast. It's not exactly where we want to go but it gets us out of here."

We got a taxi to a huge old warehouse that looked forbidding in the dark.

"I told them we were too broke to pay for a fare so try and look destitute," William said as he confidently led us inside.

"Should be easy enough under the circumstances," I grumbled.

The depot was surprisingly busy for the time of night. After they sized William up he was given the job of taking appliances off the pallets they were delivered to the depot on and packing them tightly in a truck. It was a two or three-day delivery run, and it meant the company could run one truck instead of two for the cost of a few hours packing at each end.

I watched for a while then started helping him put packing rugs between items that were not covered to prevent them scratching each other, sometimes holding them in place while he strapped larger pieces to the truck body. I put lighter objects on top of bulky ones if it was clear they wouldn't rattle around, and filled holes where I could.

"The tighter we can pack it, the less likely things are to move and damage themselves," William said.

I asked him why he was good at it.

"Packing equipment into trucks is important in the Army. You don't want explosive objects banging together unexpectedly."

We worked in silence for a while, allowing our minds to unwind.

"How did Laura know my number and why did she tip us off?" I asked. "How did you know she would help us draw the agents away?"

"That reminds me," William said. "Turn your phone off now. We had better get you a new SIM as soon as possible. I gave Laura your number as I don't have a phone myself and she asked for a contact number one afternoon when I was working at her place. I didn't see any harm in it and I'm grateful I did now."

A forklift put the next pallet on the back of the truck, spurring William back to work, but he continued answering my questions.

"Goodwill and friendship can be very important to people who are poor, they don't have much else, and I am often surprised where I find them. However, in some poor communities I have passed through, they have turned on each other. The dog-eat-dog mentality is awful.

"The park we stayed at was not unusual, by and large, and represents the other extreme, where the inhabitants help each other out to survive and they have developed a strong sense of community. In similar circumstances, the difference between being motivated by cooperation instead of competition creates communities as different as day and night. They may seem like nosey busybodies, but they look out for one another. In this case that means us too. They are good people, regardless of their circumstances, because they choose to be."

Toward the end of the shift a burly guy turned up to make sure the packing was going okay. He looked over what we had done and just nodded, which seemed like high praise. He worked next to William, yelling at the forklift driver to get off his butt and move the pallets faster. He kept pushing the pace and William kept step with him in a friendly contest. Together they managed to finish before the shift ended, both sweating heavily.

After the last box was stacked he shook hands with William, introducing himself as Jim.

"I didn't think we would get this done and I would have to leave it for the day shift, as well as holding the truck and driver up. If you are ever back here and need a job, call in."

He checked with Ian, the driver of the truck we were getting a ride in, how soon he was leaving, and as there was a bit of time, he took William off to get a shower. I was grateful as I would be the one sitting beside him.

We left as the sun was rising and drove north, stopping in Cheyenne for breakfast before turning west on I-80. A waitress at the truck stop welcomed Ian by name with a friendly smile. Obviously, he was a regular. William and I had followed him in.

"Jim was very happy with your work. He said I could put a meal or two for both of you on my expense card as a thank you so help yourself; it's on the company."

The truck had a sleeper cab with a small cot or bed behind the seats. The seats were not really intended for three people, so when we started off again I hopped on the bed as it was more comfortable and was quickly asleep. We didn't stop again until noon, and I woke to William shaking my shoulder as we drove into a truck stop. As we walked back to the truck, Ian opened the back to check nothing had moved. Satisfied with what he saw, we hit the road again.

William waited for me to climb in, but I stepped back.

"You had no sleep last night; it's your turn on the cot," I said.

I could see he was about to argue, but he looked at me, knowing I would not give in and not wanting to cause a scene, and assented. He was asleep in seconds. He is so used to looking out for himself he refuses to ever let his guard down or admit vulnerability, rely on others and let them carry some of the load.

After an hour or so, I started talking to Ian. He had been driving for nearly twelve years, and had taken loads to most parts of the US, but for him it was a just a job. I love to travel and have worked hard to earn enough money to do so when I can. He had been to all sorts of interesting places and had never bothered to look around any of them, not interested in expanding his view of the world. For me it was hard to understand.

Late in the afternoon, we skirted around Salt Lake City to head northwest on I-84. Ian said we would stop in an hour or two as he would need to take a break to sleep. William and I would need to fend for ourselves, but if we had the cash, he would stop in a town with a motel or something like it and he would take us on after his break. William was still asleep, but after thinking for a while I disregarded Army survival training's most important rule—always step back when they ask for volunteers to step forward—and volunteered William on his behalf. I told Ian William had experience with loading trucks and might be able to drive for him while he slept. It's not as if we could lose our way on an interstate after all. He said he would give the idea some thought.

We stopped for a break about an hour later and William woke up without being called. The change in sound as the truck slowed down was enough to disturb him and he was alert almost instantly. As we sat at a table together I brought up the idea of William driving as I could see Ian was not going to. I don't mind being pushy.

William showed Ian he had a truck license and brightened up considerably as he started reminiscing about some of his exploits with heavy vehicles, including joyriding in a tank at sixty miles an hour and accidently running over a parked Jeep. For someone who wasn't actually in the motor pool, he had managed to do some strange things. The two of them chattered on like old friends now that they had some common ground.

Ian matched each of William's exploits with several of his own and the break started to stretch on interminably, at least until I got bored.

"Mind if I cut in?" I interjected. "Enough of this bro'mitment thing," I said, though the classical reference was completely wasted on these cultural imbeciles. "I'm still feeling anxious enough to want to know what's going to happen next. Where I sleep tonight or even if I get to sleep somewhere tonight, would be a nice start."

The two men had the good sense to look contrite, even if they were annoyed at being interrupted in mid-stride about something so obviously trivial. They only took a few moments to agree William would drive for the next few hours while Ian slept on the cot. They walked back to the truck without a break in their reminiscing or their obliviousness to my presence as I trailed behind. Yes, men can only think of one thing at a time, and even then, the range of subjects is extremely limited.

William confidently climbed up to sit in the driver's seat, waited for me to buckle in, then without a hesitation started the truck and drove out onto the freeway in the deepening darkness of nightfall.

Not wanting to disturb Ian, we didn't talk, so I curled up on the seat as best I could but wasn't able to sleep. As time passed I stretched over to lay a hand on William and was surprised to sense that he was thinking about when he was heading west, not long after he escaped from Fort Bragg, and feeling sad. There was a momentary sense of equal surprise in William's mind as he noticed me.

Don't stop. Just go back to where we had left off, I thought. I could sense him considering then a reply that meant *okay*.

This was something new—a two-way dialogue on equal terms. In the past, I had just been a passive recipient of what William showed me, and as I look back I am amazed at how casually we simply accepted it and continued as if it were nothing out of the ordinary. Maybe, under the circumstances, it wasn't.

With no destination in mind, William drove up from Fort Bragg toward Raleigh, seeking a crowd large enough to lose himself in the impersonal loneliness of a large city. He knew the hunt for him could be underway already, but had no plan of what to do. His wallet was in his pocket, but it was empty of US money as he had been imprisoned on the base since returning from the Middle East. The idea of abandoning the car disturbed him as it offered a modicum of sanctuary in an alien place. But he knew they would be looking for it too, besides which, it would need gas and therefore money soon if he decided to keep using it. He rejected the thought of going to a bank as any transaction would pinpoint him in seconds if they were watching his accounts.

By the time he reached the city he had steeled himself to get rid of the car as quickly as possible. He drove to a Salvation Army distribution center and walked in with his lieutenant's uniform looking spick and span. He spoke to the manager saying his squad had come home from a tour of duty and they all were collecting clothes and other things they could take back for some of the refugees in a camp near their base. He asked for donations of any items that were not good enough to go on the sale racks. He was deluged with clothing that, on the whole, wasn't too bad. He thanked the man profusely for his generosity and before he left managed to pick out a good-sized backpack with a rip down one side that had been thrown in the dumpster.

He moved to a park and went through the clothing gingerly, looking for anything that would fit him and folding it carefully into the pack. He kept a set of clothes out and drove to a tourist information bureau for his last act as a US Ranger. He told them he was in the city for some rest and relaxation before shipping out and asked for a list of sites to see. He accepted all their suggestions and pamphlets with gratitude, and as an apparent afterthought, he asked innocently if there were any areas that a soldier in uniform should avoid. While the girl didn't want to be insensitive she showed him on her map where what she called the downbeat part of town was and suggested he might want to stay away from there.

She had given him his next step, but on the way he went into a mall restroom to change clothes. There were no shoes, so he had to wear his army boots, but the faded jeans he had chosen mostly hid them. He couldn't face the complete break with his past abandoning his uniform would suggest and folded it to fill the gap in his pack.

When he reached his destination, he circled the streets, finding the most battered-looking street and parked the Dodge, leaving it unlocked with the keys in the ignition. Slinging the pack on his back, he walked away without a backward glance knowing all trace of the car that had served him well and its connection to him would almost certainly be gone by morning, it might even be nothing but spare parts, but to him this felt like another betrayal of his honor.

With nowhere to go, William walked. When he was tired he rested, then he walked some more, reaching the CBD some unremembered time during the night. He fell asleep draped over his pack, only to be moved on by a police patrol. For the first time in his life William was completely free.

Unfortunately, the cost of freedom is not the price to gain your freedom but the cost of being totally responsible for yourself and your survival afterward. It needs to be paid for every day. William had no way to pay.

– CHAPTER 23 –

PLUMBING THE DEPTHS

WILLIAM BRUSHED over the next few months. They were dark memories best forgotten as he learned how to live on the street. Even so, I caught fleeting glimpses of many events as he sorted through for what he thought might be relevant.

During his first night in a homeless shelter he sat on a bunk in a large room, stitching up the rip in the side of his pack, using a borrowed needle and thread and a torn piece of denim from someone's old jeans. Suddenly, there was a shadow as a big man stood over him.

"That's my bunk."

William got up and took his pack to another bunk, then as he returned to get the clothes he had emptied out while he worked on the pack, the man tossed them over the floor. William picked up his clothes silently, sat down on the new bunk, picked up his pack and returned to his repair job.

Immediately the man was looming over him again demanding an apology. William sighed to himself as he faced the fact that the man was a bully and would not stop.

This guy has no idea how vulnerable he is, William thought as he sat looking straight at the man's groin.

William pushed his pack away gently with his left hand, jabbed with the stiff fingers of his right hand into the man's solar plexus, driving back and upward into his diaphragm. As the man doubled over, bringing his head down to William's level, William caught him by the throat with his now empty left hand and pulled his right back, bunched tightly in a fist. The man understood, but could only shake his head pleadingly as he was still unable to draw a breath. William pushed him away and went back to his sewing without uttering a word.

The violence was the antithesis of the peace William had experienced, and in his mind served to emphasize his increasing separation from it. He was no longer troubled at the shelter, but as word spread in the shadow world there were a few that wanted to try him out. William was soon left alone as the powerbrokers realized he had no ambitions to carve out his own fiefdom in their corner of the sandbox.

When he was desperate for food he sold his precious uniform to a street trader for the price of a few meals. If there is a stairway to heaven, each incident seemed to William a step in the opposite direction, and he could not free himself of the anger and resentment he felt toward his fate. He sometimes missed the helping hands and moments of fellowship that came his way. Depression and that malevolent, overriding fear hovered in the dark recesses of his mind, ready to engulf him anytime he dropped his guard.

About two to three months later, anxiety started building in his mind again. Wanting to turn his back on all he had left behind and live a normal life, he dismissed the feelings as paranoia and ignored them as they became more insistent. By this stage he was living in a boarding house as he had a laboring job at a building site and he needed to stay nearby as he didn't have a car. As he walked up the third flight of stairs to his room his instincts were screaming *danger* or *run*, but he angrily refused to acknowledge the feelings, thinking *I will not be part of that world again.*

He shoved the door open and slammed it behind him to vent his anger before realizing there were two MPs sitting in the room, Tweedledum and Tweedledee, Argus's pet gorillas. Both had guns with long silencers aiming carelessly in William's general direction and were on opposite sides of the room so either one could cover him however he moved. William was regretting having slammed the door on any chance of escape when the ape lounging on William's small bed announced derisively, "Major Jonson would like us to convey to you his disrespects."

One of them tossed William a set of handcuffs.

"Put these on," waiting to see them squeeze up before either of them were willing to drop their aim or move toward him.

One of them grabbed his shoulder, while the other went to the door and opened it, looking into the corridor before stepping out and beckoning his partner to follow. They got to the first flight of stairs and paused.

"Wait with him," the man in the front said as he walked to the bottom, turned and stepped back to cover William with his gun. William walked down the stairs in front of his comrade.

This pattern was repeated at the next flight but when they got to the last flight a young woman was climbing up and Tweedledum stepped back from the edge rather than pushing past her, an act of politeness that was his undoing.

William was close behind him when he stepped back to the top step and leapt forward, twisting to hit Tweedledum in the middle of his back with his shoulder. As he bounced off the hapless soldier, William grabbed the handrail with both hands and vaulted over, hitting the floor hard but absorbing the impact into a roll that he tried to aim toward the foot of the stairs. He was coming back on to his feet as Tweedledum tumbled to the bottom of the stairs toward William's feet, still holding the gun though with no aim in mind and struggling to come to his own feet. With no thought of remorse, William clubbed him with a wild swing from both hands as they were chained together, dropping to his knees to scramble for the gun as it fell from the man's hands when he slumped against William. William was half crouched behind Tweedledum when Tweedledee almost reached the bottom of the stairs with his own gun ready and William swung the pilfered gun to face him.

William gave him no time to think.

"I will shoot you now if you don't drop the gun."

Seeing nothing but implacable determination on William's face, he complied, and William made him kick it down the rest of the stairs. William picked it up too and put it in his pocket; the length of the silencer made the pistol grip hang out.

"I am not stupid enough to search the two of you for the key for these handcuffs with you standing over me so unless you can produce them immediately I will have to shoot you anyway." The man went pale as he sensed William had been pushed to his limit and would do as he said without hesitation. He very carefully rummaged through one of his pockets and came up with a set of keys, which he tossed as carefully to William. William made him turn and kneel on the stairs facing upward before he tried the keys to get the right one to open the cuffs. He stepped back and made Tweedledee haul his partner all the way back to his third-floor room.

William knew he had to run again but at the same time the thought of being destitute once more was something he didn't want to face. The only alternative he could see was to keep the MPs in his room while he threw his belongings into his pack. He made the conscious MP spread his feet wide, lean at a steep angle with his forehead against the wall and his fingers interlaced through the back of his belt, a position very hard to move quickly from. By the time William finished the other man, who had moved and groaned occasionally, started trying to get up.

William had his pack on one shoulder and one of the guns in his free hand as Tweedledee groaned and slumped to the floor, his muscles finally giving up the struggle to hold him up. William was expecting it and let him be.

He lifted the gun to hit the stirring Tweedledum on the back of his head and hesitated. Watching from the floor Tweedledee raised his eyebrows.

"If I hit him again so soon after the last time it is much more likely to cause permanent damage to his brain. I don't know what to do," William said.

"I understand you need time to get away, but Ron has been my friend for many years. I appreciate your considering him. Handcuff us together and I will guarantee you fifteen minutes before I raise the alarm. I give you my word of honor, it's the best I can do."

William could sense he was telling the truth and was surprised by the clarity with which he saw the man's inner intentions. William threw him the handcuffs.

"Do it yourself, but before you do, throw me his set of keys."

The other man smiled. "I will keep my word to give you your fifteen minutes, but you understand, I still want the strongest hand I can play," he said as he retrieved the keys.

"My name's Daniel by the way."

"Of course I understand," William said. "I would do the same in your position. Now I think you had better thread the cuffs behind the radiator pipe before you put it on your wrist."

He waited until his command had been obeyed, lowered the gun and gave the man a respectful salute then slipped quietly out and closed the door.

I thought to William, *So this is why you are so OCD about always keeping your pack prepared and ready.* I could sense his amusement as he thought back.

That's one way to put it I guess.

Why did you salute him as you left? I asked as it seemed so incongruous given the situation.

William went back to the memory of vaulting over the banister rail.

Daniel could have shot me in the back easily enough when I first moved, and he would have been in a much stronger position if he had stayed where he was and shot me as I hit the floor. He came down the stairs to help his partner when he knew there was probably a loose gun floating around. He is not a natural killer. Looking at him as an MP you tend to see an insensate hulk and I had thought of him that way too, but I saw that underneath all that lies a man of honor. I was letting him know that I respect him even though he is an adversary, or maybe just that I know who he really is. Regardless of that, if I crossed paths with him again I wouldn't expect any mercy.

William walked briskly down the street knowing he could trot easily but that would draw the attention of any passing police. He could feel the minutes trickle away but had not been expecting this and had no plan in mind. He saw a taxi on the other side of the street and stepped onto the road and yelled. The cab did a quick U-turn and stopped at William's feet. He tossed his pack onto the back seat and slid in himself, closing the door.

"Where to, pal?" the cabbie asked, catching William by surprise.

Where to indeed? William thought.

After a few moments of panicky deliberation, inspiration struck him.

"I need to hitch a ride west. Could you drop me off at a freeway interchange or someplace like that?"

"There's a truck stop not too far from here. As those guys are on the road at this time of night, you'd probably have the best chance if I took you there."

"Sounds good," William said.

"What you doing out at this time of night?" the cabbie asked. He was obviously bored and wanted to talk. It was probably a slow shift at this time of night.

"I just had a bust-up with my girl," William improvised. "I have family in Memphis that will put me up till we sort it out or I know we can't."

William asked the driver of every truck that appeared to be going in the right direction for a lift and was turned down a number of times, including one abusive driver who wanted nothing to do with hobos and advised him very descriptively to get a job and get a life. Still he was feeling close to elated. The extreme internal distress refusing to follow his intuition had generated was gone and he was no longer feeling torn in two. He was homeless again, only had a small amount of money left in his wallet from his last pay. It did not matter in the least. The relief at finally obeying his inner drive to leave and move west was so intense it made any other concerns pale by comparison.

While he had, with his usual extreme stubbornness and tenacity, attempted to deny and refute or expunge his past, his past was not about to forget him. Seeing this clearly, he committed himself to accepting his fate with dignity and working to make the most of what it had given him.

– CHAPTER 24 –

GETTING BACK ON THE HORSE

IT TOOK LESS THAN AN HOUR for William to get a lift west. Unfortunately, it was a short haul load that was only going as far as Salem. The driver dropped William off as he left the interstate in the early hours of the morning. William asked to be dropped off at the nearest supermarket. He had enough money for food for a few days but intended to make it last as long as possible. He walked back the three miles to the freeway and waited by the west bound onramp, hitching a ride. It took him all day and another two rides to get as far as Nashville.

It was early evening and William started walking around the restaurants, offering to wash dishes for the evening in return for a meal. It was one of the ways he had learned to get by in Raleigh. Eventually he was given a job for the evening at a restaurant that was part of a nationwide chain.

He worked hard and did a good job. At the end of the evening the manager had him fed well and afterward offered him the job. William thought for a moment and could not feel any sense of urgency.

"I will if you can find me a place to stay."

The manager yelled through the restaurant that was empty of patrons to the staff who were cleaning up before leaving.

"Can anyone put William up for the night?"

One of the assistant chefs, Rudi, whose bench was near where William had worked at the sink for the night, volunteered.

Rudi was the son of German immigrants who apparently had a flair for choosing unfortunate names for their children. He had been trained as a Michelin Chef for five-star restaurants and hated turning out cheap convenience food. One evening when Rudi cooked an exquisite *cordon bleu* meal for William at home, he put far more of the cooking wine into himself than in the cooking. William suspected that was the reason he was not a chef at a top restaurant. William got on well with him regardless, and Rudi said he could stay if he wanted.

William was paid cash nightly, not a lot, but as he was being fed as well, he built up a meager cash reserve. About a week later the feeling of unease returned. William accepted it and took some time to explore further. Any mental connection seemed to work both ways and William sensed Argus knew he was in the Nashville area. William took his pack with him for the nightshift, said his goodbyes at the end of work and moved on.

Hitching rides is never as easy at night, but William always seemed to manage it. He said he preferred nighttime because if he was lucky, after the usual pleasantries, the driver would ignore him and he could get some sleep without having to pay for a room or needing to stay semi-alert as he would when he slept rough. Alternatively, drivers would pick him up as they wanted someone to talk to help keep them awake. He enjoyed this too as he met many memorable characters, some who, under other circumstances, could have become friends.

William looked very downbeat in his old clothes and battered pack and this made it harder to get rides. Once someone picked him up and realized he was articulate and well-mannered he got on well. He had intended to stay on I-80 and continue, most likely, to LA as it took him just about as far from Argus as he could get, but the driver who took him into Memphis, Ben, offered to take him up to St Louis in two days' time when he'd finished his business in Memphis.

After he was dropped off in the city, William spent a little of his hard-earned money on an epic-sized novel from a secondhand store and walked to the bus station. Finding a spot where the seats in the lounge met in a corner, he opened the book on the table in front of him, leaned his head on his pack and happily went to sleep, knowing, with security cameras operating, he was completely safe and, looking like someone waiting for a connection, no one bothered him.

He woke late in the night, took his pack to the toilet cubicle and got out the two pistols. He weighed them for feel in his hand, and swiftly disassembled and reassembled them before choosing one. He put this one back in his pack and the other in the front of his trousers, checking very carefully that the safety was on. He put his pack in a locker and went prowling the underworld. By sunrise he had the name of a dealer who could be trusted to buy the gun without asking awkward questions, and he visited the store to sell it once the city woke up.

He used some of the money to buy a better set of clothes and get his shaggy hair cut. He hung out in the city for a while till he got bored, then visited one of the city museums, found a quiet corner to sit down and went to sleep.

You are a total Philistine, I thought at him. *In the middle of Fidelio, you would just see a fat lady singing.*

That's true, he countered happily, *what's your point? Besides, I couldn't pull the same stunt at the bus station two nights in a row.*

William returned to the bus station late in the evening, leaving it as late as he could and retrieved his pack before the locker hire ran out. He showered and shaved then wandered off to find a café to wait out the rest of the night. He started reading the book.

He turned up at the meeting place an hour early to make sure he didn't miss his ride. To pass the time as he waited, he tried meditating, something he hadn't attempted since escaping, but for all his efforts, he was not able to prevent his mind wandering. His unwavering attempt to still his mind just felt like holding his head in a vice, an act of aggression that produced no sense of peace at all. He struggled to banish the disappointment from his mind knowing that wallowing in it, giving in to bitterness or regret, would simply lead him back to depression.

Old habits die hard, if at all, and once William stopped fighting or trying to control the process, his training took over. When Ben picked him up William had turned all his attention to his body, simply feeling his breath come in and out, gradually expanding his attention to the other sensations in and around him. He still did it with his usual total commitment, but it was an act of acceptance, living in the moment without reference to the past or future. It was a start.

The trip to New Orleans went well. When they arrived, Ben took William to the restaurant he usually frequented. The owner welcomed Ben warmly and after they had finished, sat down at the table to chat with him. Ben introduced William, repeating the little information William had given and surprised William by finishing with, "I don't know the story but he's a good guy and could use a break. Can you give him a job?"

The owner thought for a moment and then asked, "You look like you can handle yourself. Can you?" William admitted he could if he needed to. The owner offered William a job as doorman at his cousin's nightclub and suggested Ben take him over when they left. Consequently, William started his new and promising career as a bouncer at a dodgy club in New Orleans. As part of the deal, the owner gave William a small room on the top floor for a very moderate rent.

During the morning, the front door to the club was locked so William was given a key to come and go through the back door which also served as the emergency fire exit into the alley behind. Walking out the first time he noticed a sign for an aikido club outside one of the buildings and resolutely ignored it. His intuition had other ideas and each time he passed the push to enter was stronger, but he resisted simply out of bloody-mindedness. He had capitulated within a week and surrendered to what he could see was the inevitable. He went in, checked out the training times and was back at the dojo the next time it fitted in with his schedule.

He didn't like the style particularly and had to remind himself each class of the steps he considered important. Centering and grounding, then breathing and relaxation—elements of living in your own body properly before you even consider dealing with the world around you. Performing the *Tai-Sabaki* over and over again to refine and ingrain them. Doing each tiny part of a technique correctly and with full concentration, without seeing the finish as particularly important or something to be rushed to.

Perhaps it was important these basics were not emphasized as it forced William to take responsibility for them himself. He was having to reteach himself that it doesn't matter what or how much you know; it doesn't matter how important or special you think you are. It's what you do, actually put into practice, day after boring day, that counts.

CHAPTER 25

LAST TANGO IN USA

I SUDDENLY WOKE UP, realizing I had fallen asleep. The monotonous drone of the truck continued unabated, but it felt like I had been asleep forever, so I leaned over William to look at the clock on the truck dashboard. It was just after midnight and I groaned in disgust.

"Awake, are we?" William commented dryly. "Wasn't boring you, was I?"

"Of course, William," I replied. "Your life has been so mind-numbingly dull and uninteresting, unconsciousness seemed a fascinating experience by comparison."

He snorted disdainfully.

"Get some more sleep if you can; the highway branches off north to Seattle somewhere ahead and I think we will part company with Ian there."

"How far away?" I asked.

"Four or five hours I would guess."

"So why do we need to get off the truck?"

"Well, it's always a good idea never to go to the end of a ride. If there are people waiting for you, they never know where you got off. Besides, we need to be heading toward LA and that's the opposite direction to Seattle, so it makes sense anyway."

"You're that keen to get rid of me?"

"The sooner the better," he said, but I knew it was because he didn't think I was safe here anymore, officially an accomplice to his crimes now.

I couldn't go back to sleep, probably because I had been told I should, so I sat up. Watching the lights of cars go by in the dark soon lost its appeal. I leaned against William and relaxed. Shortly I could sense the presence of his thoughts.

Shall we continue? I suggested.

We were suddenly back in his room in New Orleans. The feeling of menace was back, and he knew the noose was tightening again. It was time to move on. There was a strong feeling of regret as he had been getting on well.

"How long has it been?" I questioned.

"Almost two months, the longest time I have been left alone by them since I got out of Raleigh."

He had told his boss he might have to leave unexpectedly sometime before, so there was no surprise when he said he had to go.

As he had some money in reserve now and also didn't feel like the stress of hitching when his pursuers were close, he paid for a Greyhound to Kansas City. On a whim, he left the interstate there and decided to hitch across the state, going wherever his rides took him, stopping if he could get work, moving on if he couldn't, a genuine drifter living with the homeless and dispossessed. The only condition was his need to keep moving west.

It took him months, later moving north into Nebraska then turning west again into Wyoming, but he was never in one place for more than a week. By the time he reached Cheyenne he was tired of constantly moving and wanted the running over, to be able to establish himself somewhere. He took a Greyhound again, this time all the way to the west coast, to San Francisco.

As I saw this and looked a little deeper I realized William had been feeling a sense of futility rather than sadness earlier. When we covered the first stretch of our trip to Salt Lake City in the truck with Ian yesterday, we were following the same road William had taken in the bus from Cheyenne. William had come full circle. He was retracing his steps and he was still running. It had seemed worse this time to him as he felt he had more to lose. Driving north from Salt Lake City broke the pattern and William had quickly shaken the feeling or was working on that when I joined his mind.

William had saved as much as he could from his work and so nosed around the streets until he found a cheap room in San Francisco. He started training again in an inner-city dojo with some great instructors, but in a month his instincts told him it was time to move on.

William decided to travel north over the Golden Gate and worked his way up the coast on Highway 101. He almost got as far as Oregon, returning to his drifter lifestyle as he was hounded on anytime he became settled, before his instincts suggested he needed to go south. The hunt seemed to be intensifying and William turned back, moving inland and from city to city as fate demanded.

Reaching San Diego, he could go no further without a passport. William stayed as long as he could, playing a cat-and-mouse game with unseen opponents, uncertain what to do next. Finally, he gave up and returned north, making his way back to Los Angeles. Twice he moved when inner promptings told him agents were near, but he could sense no purpose or direction to move on. Feeling abandoned, he decided to test whether his promptings were true.

He waited when he sensed agents were on the way to his latest lair and hid nearby, determined to see if they would actually come. He saw two men arrive in an unmarked car and walk somewhat hesitantly into the hobo enclave where he had found sanctuary for the last few days. He felt safe in his hiding place thinking they would find him gone and would return to their base to get new orders or to wait till Argus next sensed where William was staying. He watched as both agents ran back out of the alley. One leapt into the driver's seat and started the car; the other was holding a mobile phone to his ear and turning his head to look wildly up and down the street. His gaze steadied when he identified the old building where William was watching from a stairwell window on the third floor. He pointed and jumped in the car.

William cursed and ran down the passage leading from the stairwell to the back of the building, hoping to find the fire escape. There was no way the agents could have seen him, but he knew they knew he was there. If he ran down the stairs he would reach the front doors at about the same time the agents did. He found a fire escape door and it creaked open when he leaned his weight against it. Reaching the ground, he ran with his pack, not caring if he drew attention as he already had more attention than he could cope with.

William ran for the commercial streets where there would be lots of people. While the men would have old photos of him, he did not look anything like that now. As he had moved he had regularly changed his look, different combinations of long hair, short hair, hair colors, beards, glasses or sunglasses, even changing how he walked and held himself. He was sure he could disappear once he was in a crowd.

He slowed down as the crowds thickened and he ran out of breath from running. Seeing people waiting for a bus he squeezed onto one end of the seat to sit down, reflecting angrily to himself that not so long ago, when he was a Ranger, he could have run half a day like that. When the bus arrived a few moments later, he just followed the others on without thinking. When you want to be part of a group you follow it if it moves.

After paying the driver, he turned and looked down the bus. I should have been expecting it, but I was still surprised when I realized it was me his eyes settled on. He was still thinking strategically, and he instantly saw the empty seat beside me and saw me as a way to blend in, while I was thinking, *Is that what I look like?*

For some reason that effect where two mirrors face each other crossed my mind. I wondered if we could get an infinite series with our minds connected, me watching William watch me watch him watch me ad infinitum. William's thoughts disappeared abruptly.

"Don't even think about it," he blurted.

"Hey," I complained, "that could have been fun."

"It twists my head inside out just trying to imagine it. Don't try it, not now, not ever. You and your ideas of fun," he said.

I told him he was a boring old fart.

"But you love me anyway," he laughed.

"Don't take that too far," I suggested for his benefit.

"So what happened after you got off the bus?" I continued. "Did you think about me?"

"Not at all," he answered with typical masculine insensitivity; or is it stupidity?" I moved around for an hour or two then sat in the middle of a city park once I knew I had lost them, somewhere reasonably hidden where I couldn't be seen easily from a road, but I could see anyone coming from any direction. That night I went to a mission on the east side of the city that deals with the homeless and got a bed for the night. During the night, I made up my mind to go east, possibly Texas, and left as soon as I could to hitch an early morning ride. The rest you know."

He drifted off into silence.

We still were some way from the junction, and I did doze off for another hour or two. I woke when William touched me on the arm before calling out to Ian to wake up. Once he was lucid William told him we would get out when we reached the interstate. He was a little surprised.

"There's only Hermiston there; it's the middle of nowhere."

He showed William where to turn off before the junction, so we stopped in the middle of the little town where we said goodbye to Ian.

We hung around, waiting for the sun to rise. William said two people together had a better chance of thumbing a ride when it was daylight, so there was not a lot of point rushing back to the freeway.

"I know I have been calling the shots again but it's because we are playing a game only I have experience with. I feel a bit guilty to be ordering you around, but we haven't had other choices. So what I want to do is hitch a ride to Portland, then get buses from there to LA."

"We are in Oregon, aren't we?" I asked.

"Yes, just south of the Washington state line," he said suspiciously, obviously wondering what I was cooking up.

"Okay, isn't Crater Lake in Oregon? Can we visit? It is one of the things I was considering doing but I didn't think I would be getting this far north."

I could tell he was wavering.

"Please!" I wheedled sweetly, at the risk of severe damage to my self-respect.

He sighed and started digging in his pack, finally coming up with a small sheaf of tourist maps. Leafing through, he came up with one of Oregon.

"I never made it this far, so I'll have to see if it's possible.

"It looks like it's a long way from anywhere. I wouldn't like to try hitching there in a hurry, particularly with two of us."

I made no comment but waited expectantly, broadcasting my confidence in William's ability to overcome such a tiny problem.

He acquiesced.

"I guess we could stop off at The Dalles and see if it's possible to get to Crater Lake from there," he said diffidently.

"Sounds like a plan then," I agreed.

When it was light enough we walked a couple of miles back to the interstate and were lucky to get a ride quickly. Even so, it took us another two lifts, so it was late afternoon by the time we booked into a backpackers in The Dalles. We went to our room to drop our packs where I suggested we have an early dinner as we had not had a lot to eat. William said he would like to go walking first.

He pulled his gun out of his pack and fished around a little longer to get the silencer and some spare ammunition. He put it in a carry bag, looked at the silhouette of the gun that could be clearly seen, then wrapped it in a magazine and put it back in the bag.

"Let's go."

It didn't take long to reach the river, and we walked along till there was a moment when there were no people nearby. William stopped, turned to the river and with a step threw the bag with the gun. He stood gazing for a time at the spot where it had disappeared with an unremarkable splash into the dark, cold waters of the Columbia River. Satisfied, he walked back to me and took my hand to continue walking as if it were just another everyday event in our lives, but I stopped him.

"Why did you do that?"

"Long answer or short answer?"

"Long I guess."

"Okay, I guess I'm stating who I am. As a race, we have chosen warfare as our basic form of interaction. Whether it's invading other countries to steal their resources, using multinationals or franchises or whatever to legally steal their money because it looks better and is cheaper, needing a bigger car or to be prettier to prove I am better than someone else, the principle is the same. By carrying a gun, I am both consciously and tacitly saying I am willing to be part of that way of living. I have decided I am not willing to continue doing that anymore or support that view of the world. If I honestly want peace I have to choose it in every way I can, not just where it is convenient. Throwing the gun away is something I should have done a long time ago."

Hitchhiking had proved to be too slow and challenging. The next morning William decided to rent a car using one of his aliases. He knew it was risky, but we were nearing the end of our journey and he figured we could stay ahead of our pursuers by moving quickly from place to place.

We spent the night at Crater Lake, then walked up Mt. Lassen the next day. We took our time, crisscrossing between states, visiting Lake Tahoe, Yosemite and Death Valley. We passed the giant redwoods over the next couple of days before staying at Palmdale for our last night.

I asked William if he was going to hang around while I booked a flight and waited for it as my ticket was open and it could take a few days.

"As soon as your name comes up on an outgoing flight it will alert somebody somewhere and I would almost guarantee military agents will turn up as you board the flight. They might even stop you from leaving. What I think we should do is drop you at the airport and for you to go to the Air New Zealand counter and tell them you have just heard from your family your father is desperately ill, heart attack or whatever you like, and you need to get home as soon as you can. They should put you on standby, waiting to see if there are any seats from no-shows left on planes as they leave. You won't be on the passenger list until the plane is ready to leave."

Of course, my anxiety levels went through the roof and it was not a happy evening for either of us though William took me out to dinner and did everything he could to cheer me up.

The morning came and after breakfast William quietly drove us to LA airport. He drove to the drop-off area for international departures and got my pack out of the boot as I found a trolley and brought it back. He put my pack on the trolley then hugged me.

"I won't come in and wait with you. When your name hits the computer system I want to be as far away from here as possible."

He reached out with his mind to brush mine and I answered. He promised me again in a way I could see there were no reservations and only honesty that if it was humanly possible, he would come to me.

"Go," he said kindly, and waited for me to start pushing the trolley away.

I turned when I heard the door slam and the grief welled up as I watched him drive away. He may still feel like he has lost so much, but I could see in him what he was unable or unwilling to see in himself yet. The circumstances have not changed but he was no longer running or perceiving himself as a victim; he was resolute and strong but with that inner core of gentleness. He may not be proud of where he was—the maelstrom he was caught in—but he was proud once again, in a way that had nothing to do with narcissistic egotism, of himself. It was truly a victory.

CHAPTER 26

HOME

THINGS WORKED OUT pretty much as William predicted. The check-in lady looked at her schedules.

"We don't have a plane leaving till this afternoon, but there is a Qantas flight on final boarding."

She phoned them and they had a seat so I was rushed through the departure formalities. It meant I had to fly to Sydney and get another flight from there to Auckland, but I didn't care. They let me call my parents from a phone in the departure lounge and I was on my way. My parents picked me up from the airport and I returned with them to my family home in Taumarunui.

After a week's moping around I went up to see my friends where I used to work, and the manager offered me my old job back, so I moved up to Hamilton and started work. There are a couple of dojos there and I chose one and got back into training. It didn't feel right without William, but I knew he hadn't given up and neither would I.

"The whole point of relentless training and discipline is to achieve a state of spontaneity that lets us act in a way that's totally appropriate to any situation—the opposite of regimentation," one instructor said. "It's an oxymoron, a complete contradiction in terms. The value of any discipline that helps us on is whether or not it increases our awareness of what is really happening, particularly in our own mind."

On another night he commented, "Many people are just replaying a looped program in their heads, outputting their rigidly inflexible judgments and opinions to any new situation that arises. They have ceased to be creative or alive in any real sense."

What it added up to for me was: pay attention.

The weeks turned into months and there was still no sign from William, but I knew he was still there. I would have known if he was in trouble or had changed his mind. After four and a half months my dad received a cryptic postcard from Hawaii.

Thinking of you and all is well.

He showed it to me on my next visit home because he had no idea who it was from or what it was really saying. I knew before I touched it that it was from William. I hoped he was on his way.

I spent some time trying to tell Mum and Dad about this guy I had met while I was in the US and why he couldn't come visit me in the usual way. I disclosed that he might have been chased by government agents and he may be coming to New Zealand, but I didn't know for sure.

A month or so later I knew William was thinking of me or he was nearby, I wasn't sure which, and within a week my mum phoned to say a strange man calling himself William was there asking to see me. This made sense as I had given him my parents' address, not having one of my own.

"Don't let him leave," I commanded, "even if you have to tie him down."

Our reunion was as happy as I had hoped. William was suitably nervous and on his best behavior as I officially introduced him but had been getting on rather well on his own. We stayed the night before going away for a few days for my own peace of mind.

In a way, it was all reversed. This time it was my car and I was taking him where I wanted. William had changed his wardrobe and was the not-so-proud owner of a new, very tidy pack.

"Look, William," I teased, "you've been through hell and back but everywhere you went, in every experience you showed me, your loyal old backpack was always there for you.

"You often changed your look but if the security heads had had any brains, the agents would have been told to look for the pack. They would have known you anywhere."

He laughed.

"You have abandoned all you stood for," I insisted. "It was the symbol of your rejection of all concerns with status and the trappings of material success, but here you are, looking like the furthest you've been into the wilderness is an expensive sporting store and the most traumatic thing you've ever faced was paying the bill."

I was enjoying myself.

"Ah, how I've missed you," he finally said. "The best thing I can do is show you, so you'll just have to wait."

Later, when we were alone in the evening, he touched my mind.

Want to see what happened to me after you left the US?

Of course, I thought back.

William was driving east from LA airport, intending to get out of California, when he had the feeling he was going the wrong way. He turned back and eventually made his way to the warehouses around the docks in LA. He hung around and got a job after a few days as a laborer for one of the port companies. A couple of weeks later one of the shift supervisors offered William a job with his brother, who had a couple of fishing boats working out of San Diego.

William learned fast, and soon fit in well with the fishing boat crew. They were a hard bunch, but he enjoyed the camaraderie of being back in a situation where he had to depend on his mates and they could depend on him. He tended to hang out with them after work and when they had days off and, as a result, mixed with the people they mixed with. Most importantly this included the crews of the big private yachts when they were in port, which was a lot of the time for some of them. William decided this was a way he could get out of the States undetected, but first he would need a passport so he could get into other countries. He had saved as much of his wages as he could and over time had figured out who to approach in the underworld to get a passport in another man's name. He still had to work some other dangerous and possibly illegal jobs and do some favors for unsavory people.

When he had what he wanted he told some of his acquaintances he was bored and was thinking about crewing on a yacht if it was going anywhere interesting. He got a fill-in job on a yacht to Hawaii. To keep his clothes dry he bought an almost-new pack designed for the marine environment from one of his deck-hand friends and regretfully threw his old pack away.

In Hawaii, he volunteered to crew another boat to Fiji and from there joined a rich couple who had decided to invite another couple they knew to help sail their new yacht from Auckland. The friends had decided upon reaching Suva that flying home was a much safer prospect, leaving the owners in need of help to sail their yacht home again.

William happily took charge, having had a little experience and some good instruction during the earlier legs of his trip. He was lucky they had some good charts and a state-of-the-art GPS to tell him where he was on the charts, so he managed to find his way to Rangitoto Island and the Waitemata Harbor. Once in Auckland, he came looking for me and that meant looking up my parents.

William came with me back to Hamilton and I moved flats to accommodate him. After a couple of weeks, he got bored and hitched over to Tauranga and a job picking kiwifruit, coming back for the weekends.

One Saturday morning at training I was clearly getting frustrated with some new technique. William sidled over.

"You're wasting your energy trying to match an image you have in your head. Let it go and just watch carefully what you are doing now without trying so hard."

Later when we were working together he said, "We all learn different things at our own rates. The process stops being a burden and can be fun if we stop laying ridiculous expectations on ourselves of what we should achieve."

He started laughing at his own cleverness.

"Isn't it ironic that for a supposedly defensive martial art, we learn best when we let down or give up our defenses?"

Fate, as usual, had its own plans and a life of normality and domesticity was to be denied us once again. Sounds cool, but I still can't figure out why any self-respecting woman would choose boring domesticity anyway.

My mother called us one evening.

"There's someone here who wants to speak to William."

I handed the phone over to William, who was sitting beside me. William listened for a while then responded.

"I can't discuss it now, but I will meet you when I can. I need a number where I can call you . . . Got it."

Why would someone be at Mum's place wanting William? I thought.

William confirmed my worst fears.

"Who was that?"

"No one important," he said.

– CHAPTER 27 –
REDEMPTION

WILLIAM DIDN'T SLEEP much that night, and neither did I. I could sense his anxiety and he could sense mine. William's mind was locked down tight. He wouldn't open up to me or reassure me in any way other than verbally. He clearly didn't want me seeing his thoughts.

The next morning William was on tenterhooks waiting for me to go to work and refusing to tell me what was going on. Finally, it got too much.

"I know the drill," I yelled at him. "As soon as I am out the door you are going to slope off and deal with whatever is happening in your own way without telling me or giving me any choice."

William was adopting his neither-confirm-nor-deny stance.

"If you have to do whatever this is, I am coming with you."

"You can't," William replied softly, "it would put you in too much danger."

"Don't hand me that crap. Just knowing you has put me in danger. I am coming with you."

"And your family?" William asked, "What about them? I have no idea how this will play out. They could be caught up in it too."

"You sound just like General Ryder when you bring my family into it," I snapped.

William recoiled like I had slapped him.

"I am not threatening your family in any way," he stormed back. "I'm making sure they are not threatened. If you only knew what's happening."

What's happening is you hate arguments and you are trying to slip away rather than face me or even admit we are arguing. Stupid man. You would rather go to war and die than argue with me on even terms and, besides, I would know what was going on if you would tell me."

He politely agreed with me on all counts but added nothing more.

"I can tell wherever you are now just like you can tell where I am. I knew when you arrived in New Zealand. Anywhere you go, I can follow, and I will. You promised me you would not leave me again."

He looked crestfallen.

"Yes," he admitted. "I had forgotten that. You are right, you can come with me."

How magnanimous of him.

After some quick arranging, we went to my car.

"My car, I'm driving, and I'm going to Taumarunui. You should be very glad I have agreed to let you come with me."

I was serious, but William started laughing.

"Okay . . . okay, I get it."

We started talking as we drove down.

"There were people here from the US and they want me to meet with them. I assume they want to take me back. I have a number to contact them."

"Anyone specific?" I inquired as I could tell he wasn't telling the whole story.

"Possibly," he admitted.

"Look, if you don't behave yourself I'm going to put you out and make you walk for a while," I warned.

He smiled. "Argus is with them."

"And you didn't think this was worth mentioning earlier?"

"I wanted to avoid it because I knew it would only make you more determined."

We made it safely home and still talking to one another politely too. Mum was very surprised by our unexpected arrival and somewhat put out as she hadn't been able to prepare in her usual way. To put her at ease I said

I would pop down to the supermarket and get what she needed. I took William aside and gave him a very graphic description of the consequences if he tried to disappear on me, and left him talking to Mum and Dad.

My suspicious mind noticed a car that drove up behind me after I left our dead-end street, but then it disappeared as I crossed the bridge and turned down the main street. I did my shopping and walked back to my car with my hands full of bags. I was annoyed seeing someone lounging nonchalantly against the driver's door.

Straightening up, he turned to look at me. I recognized the face in an instant; I had seen it often enough through William's eyes.

My initial reaction was intense anger, which he obviously sensed.

"Ah, I see you recognize me; we can dispense with introductions then."

"What happens if I scream and call for the police?"

"Well, actually nothing. Officially I am here on a diplomatic mission to our embassy. I even have diplomatic immunity, which the general thoughtfully arranged. However, I need to speak to you somewhere a little more private, please."

"So you get me somewhere there are no witnesses to see your thugs kidnap me. Is that how you hope to get William to give himself up to you?"

"I have all the leverage over William I need. My associates have no idea I am talking to you and would be very upset if they knew. Ostensibly, they are here to take orders from me, but I am well aware they have their own orders that will countermand mine, which are to capture William, when the time comes. They probably aren't even here with US passports in case there is an unfortunate incident. Our noble government does have its reputation to consider. They are here to watch me as much as carry out the general's agenda. By any normal standards, the general is paranoid, and by definition suspicious of everything and everyone, particularly me at the moment as it happens.

"What's important to you is that the men are assassins. That is what they are here for. The General has decided it all ends here. He could have killed William before, but he wanted to capture him and bring him to heel—the domination game. Prove himself the better man in his own mind. Now it doesn't matter anymore. William is going to die if you don't let me help.

So what difference will it make, how much worse can it be, if you do accept my help?"

"It will make a big difference to me if William is dead and I am your slave."

"That is a little dramatic; I don't take slaves. However, if you want to save William, you will have to trust me. The decision is yours and you have no time to decide."

I took him through the underpass under the railway line and down to the old scout hall where I had learnt ballet. We sat on the grass out the back.

"Okay, convince me."

"There is nothing I can say that will convince you to trust me to the degree I need. You will have to look in my mind to truly judge my intent."

"Link minds with you," I spat, the idea was appalling. "Who would hold all the cards?"

"Me, obviously, but if it makes you feel better you can hold the gun. If you feel me do anything untoward, try to force you to do something you don't want, you can shoot me."

He pulled out a tiny gun from a shoulder holster and handed it to me.

I thought, *That's a girl's gun*, as I took it.

He said, "I know but I can't stand on my dignity. I am not allowed to carry a gun in your country, so it has to be small and discreet."

So, he can see what I am thinking, even when there is no link between our minds.

"The general insisted I bring one in case William decided to kill me instead of me forcing him to come home, at least that's what he told me. He doesn't understand who William is."

I cradled the gun for a few moments and handed it back.

"William has turned his back on force, violence like this. I would be ashamed to do less."

"You are stronger than you give yourself credit for," he said. "Now we have to do this quickly before William comes looking for you."

I felt his mind brush mine and recoiled.

"You will only trust me if you see the truth for yourself and this is the only way." I stopped fighting and relaxed as much as I could.

Shortly the thought came. *Look into my mind.*

He offered no resistance as I rifled through his memories, which showed whatever I thought about. I collected his memories faster than I could process them and had to come back to them later to sort them out.

I saw some of the terrible things he had done at General Ryder's bidding as this had been my first concern and felt his guilt and regret at the same time.

Why? I thought. Then I saw his two daughters, both teenagers now but younger in his memory of the time they were threatened, his long suffering and gentle wife, a serviceman's wife who had followed him on his postings and sacrificed her own career for his. She had been moved, along with the children, to the officers housing at Fort Bragg by General Ryder when he had discovered Argus's ability. I saw the aftermath of his last interview with William, which took him some time to recover from. His shock at his own near death and a period of soul searching leading to the growing realization he was not willing to live the way he had been coerced into any longer either. There was no retribution on Odette, Hank or Kenji for helping William escape. Argus hid their part and took the blame.

General Ryder insisted Argus pinpoint William's location after his escape, but Argus spun it out, and never gave an exact position. The general came to suspect Argus was holding out on him but has so far been unable to prove it. Argus informed the general sometime after I left the US that he could no longer locate William in the continental US.

The agents from Denver reported to General Ryder about my probable connection to William, so when William disappeared after immigration showed I had left, he assumed William had found a way to follow me. Once General Ryder knew about me and my family he knew he could force William out of hiding if enough pressure was applied. Argus was only sent in case William did not take the bait quickly enough because he could find William even if William did not want to be found.

He and Hank quickly became friends as Hank had his own ways of seeing the truth. He often relied on Hank's advice in difficult situations, including how he was handling the present situation.

Argus intruded on my interrogation thinking.

"We have to stop. William is getting restive and he will come straight to you. I would prefer he does not see me with you as he would jump to unfortunate conclusions, and awareness, not only of his thoughts but of the presence of his mind beside me, winked out."

I realized that even while I was interrogating him, Argus was keeping tabs on William as well as General Ryder's two killers, who had their own car and were around here somewhere.

"I can see how strong you really are, and it scares me. How were Hank and the others able to keep you ignorant of their plans? William was also surprised that they were able to orchestrate all the elements in his escape. Their talents were much stronger than he expected."

"I am much stronger now than I was then. William is a catalyst; his unbreakable sense of honor reminds us or brings us back to our own sense of honor. Unconsciously, he makes being less than you can be seem somehow unacceptable. William's gift lies in his great goodwill. It seems a strange thing to say, but his attitude may be more important than any talent. He respects other people for what they are and allows them to be more than they thought they could be."

"What happened to William can't really be considered a talent. It was more a different experience of reality that forced apparent reality to conform to it. I think he had the experience because he is so singularly focused and his will is so strong. Fear automatically weakens us."

As he said this, I thought, *fear and adrenaline can make us stronger.*

"Of course, for bodies it can. I am talking about minds here," Argus replied. "Isolationism is an act of fear and therefore weakens us. Inclusiveness, cooperation, goodwill all increase our strength. Hank and Kenji were stronger because William was there. He subconsciously reminded them they could be strong, particularly in that state he was in. Equally they have grown further because they chose to work together. Odette is a good healer, but could no way have done what she did if it hadn't been William there. We are all stronger too as we work together.

"William is able to heal himself because he experienced Odette heal him, and some of her talent rubbed off. The mind link developed between you and William because William had experienced direct mind-to-mind communication with me, so his mind understood it was possible. Communication rather than invasion or mind control is my real talent and some of that rubbed off on William too."

He had continued talking, even though we had reached my car, to finish his explanation.

"I don't know this country. I need to meet William somewhere very isolated but also somewhere you can see us clearly and still be hidden. That is vital."

"Piriaka Lookout," I said. "It is on the road to National Park. I think there is a road that goes off to the left just past it, but I can't remember."

"It will have to do, we are out of time," he stated curtly. "Don't tell William any of this," he commanded as an afterthought and strode off.

– CHAPTER 28 –

A RESOLUTION

I MET WILLIAM walking toward the center of town as I drove home. I stopped and leaned over to push the door open.

"You have to put your thumb out if you want a ride."

"Really?" he replied somewhat caustically, "this hitching thing is all so new to me." He said he was feeling worried about me as I was taking so long. I replied that I had bumped unexpectedly into a friend and we had got a little lost in our conversation.

I was feeling very uncomfortable needing to conceal what Argus and I discussed, and could not let William see what was on my mind. William was aware I was hiding something.

"I was worried because you seemed to have gone far away or were very hard to find. As usual, there is more to your visit to town than meets the eye."

"That's true," I replied, "but I would like you to ignore it for the meantime. Please trust me on this one."

Fear and mistrust always walk hand in hand. In the opposite corner true faith and trust can only coexist with great courage. William accepted my request without rancor or second thoughts.

For my own part I had to accept William's decision to meet Argus. In the evening William phoned the number he had been given and Argus told William to meet him on the road just past Piriaka Lookout, early in the morning.

William asked me where the lookout was and if he could borrow my car to get there. I told him I would drive him as far as the lookout and stay there. He could take the car and go the rest of the way.

He tried to argue but was overwhelmed by my determination. I made it very clear if he tried to slip away during the night I would hunt him and if I couldn't find him I would be at the rendezvous point before him. He agreed on the condition, and he was adamant that I would not come past the lookout and that I kept out of the way. Regardless, I went to sleep with my car keys in my hand, much to William's chagrin.

We left before breakfast. Neither of us was in a mood for eating. As we drove William started to explain his decision to give himself up and I made it clear I understood. Words were not necessary.

I pulled over at the lookout and we walked around the car, meeting half way. William hugged me and said some tender things, but I knew he was meaning goodbye.

As he started the car I sneaked a look over the edge and it was not how I remembered it. The side road was too far away for me to see it clearly. There was a car parked there and someone beside it, but I couldn't make out who it was. Stepping toward the edge and concealing myself as best I could in the small shrubs, I thought strongly of Argus and suddenly his mind was there, part of mine. It was nothing like the link with William where we both had to focus on each other, to make an effort to create it. It was so startling I experienced an instant panic reaction and tried to run and fight him off at the same time. He withdrew, seeming to become very small and very distant at the same time. I calmed myself and he came back.

It's too far away, I can't see clearly, I almost cried with frustration and despair.

I thought that might be the case when I checked this place out yesterday evening. You will have to use my eyes as well as your own, Argus thought back.

There was a blank moment followed by some blurring between the edges of his mind and mine and suddenly I was seeing what Argus was seeing as well as what my own eyes showed. It was disorienting, not only because of seeing double but because along with the sight I could also sense through his mind the assassins crouched behind the fences on each side of the road and knew their car was a little farther down the side road.

William turned off the main road and I sensed through Argus both agents bringing their guns up, their sense of relaxation disappearing. My mind panicked as I desperately ran through options.

Block the bullets, no, shift William away, no, shift the bullets away.

Focus, I can't do it for you, Argus thought back.

William had pulled to the side and stopped behind Argus's car. He got out and my panic and random fears were gone. I was finally riveted to the spot by what was happening. My awareness zeroed in and tiny details jumped clearly into focus. It sounds like a cliché, but time slowed down or expanded—or something.

As William was getting close to Argus both agents fired together. I saw the bullets clearly in my mind and the substance in them seemed too real; I could not stop them. My vision saw more deeply and the bullets were held together by forces that were real, but the laws that governed their strength seemed at best arbitrary—almost a matter of opinion.

I changed something (*my opinion? the bullets' opinion? the Universe's opinion?*) of how strongly they were held together, and they started to change. When they hit William, it was more like being hit with something closer to rubber bullets than lead.

One hit William square in the chest, the other from the side. There was still a lot of momentum; he was hit hard and he fell back. I was suddenly aware of what he was thinking, and seeing, and there was no surprise, only peaceful acceptance. *Damn him.* He knew something like this was going to happen and he came anyway.

He was attempting to stand again, and I thought furiously, *stay down*. This time he was surprised, both by picking up the thought and by the vehemence behind it. He stayed down.

I suddenly realized why I was sensing William's thoughts. Argus's thoughts—his help—was no longer there. I looked hard and there was still a thread of awareness connecting us. I followed it and understood.

Argus was affecting how both agents were seeing the events, controlling their minds so they thought they had seen the bullets hitting into William's body. Juggling two other minds at once required all his concentration and he had nothing left to spare for me.

The men had climbed over the fences and walked up to William. One agent aimed at his forehead, took his time and fired. As this was happening William thought, *How very textbook, always aim for a body shot, it incapacitates if it doesn't kill, you can make sure later.*

I was panicking again, desperately trying to catch Argus's attention, wanting/needing his help again.

I saw the man's finger begin to squeeze the trigger through William's eyes and went cold. Something inside me demanded *this will not happen* and, again, twisted the forces within the bullet. The rest of my mind looked on and sighed in disbelief, something like, *Oh, is that how you do it? It's so easy.*

It was still almost too late. William blanked out into unconsciousness as the bullet hit him. I was alone in my head.

I watched as the three men got into Argus's car and drove down the side road toward the agents' car. Argus popped into my mind again as he had released his control of the agents.

How is William?

Argus checked. Fine if a little damaged. He can heal himself easily enough, but you might have to remind him he is capable of doing so.

Why couldn't we tell William?

You keep seeing this in such a linear fashion. This was never about whether William was shot or not. This situation is a product of people's minds, ours, the agents, particularly the general, and I should probably throw Hank and Kenji in there too. There is great power in a focused mind and the general very much wants to see William dead. With his total self-absorption and his total commitment to power as the only morality, in his own way he is more powerful than any of us, me included. I think there is a way of looking at the world that the general and his kind represent, something that is real and alive in its own way that would dearly like to see what William stands for stamped out. William came here with dignity and true pride, not the inflated egotism that passes for pride. Integrity is power in its own right and that is William's contribution that helped events occur as they did. Any sneakiness or furtiveness if William had tried to avoid what he knew he had to do would have nullified that and changed the outcome.

He had stopped at the agents' car while they got in. I stood up, thinking it was over. Argus noticed and thought.

Stay hidden. They know about you from their briefings. If they see you and realize you saw what they did, they will kill you.

Argus turned his car around and the other car followed him back toward the main road.

What have Hank and Kenji got to do with this? I asked.

A lot. When William first arrived at Fort Bragg Hank had a very strong premonition that William would need to escape and that it would be important. He had no idea what to do and asked Kenji for help. With Kenji searching for possible ways out and Hank able to tell what the likely outcomes were, over time they were able to come up with a way for William to escape. Not only that, they have developed their own form of communication like me or you and William. Their abilities have grown stronger as they have worked together. Hank insisted William not know and that you had to do what you did by yourself.

But I didn't, I insisted. *You helped me.*

He was gone for a moment as the agents drove past William's prone body to make sure they saw it as they were supposed to. Argus turned south, heading back toward the embassy, and the agents turned north, presumably to catch the first plane out of Auckland they could get.

Argus checked to see they were on their way and stopped on the side of the road to answer my question.

Diane, he thought with a strong sense of kindness behind the words, *apart from giving you confidence, a little encouragement or direction, I did nothing. I watched what you did very carefully, and I have tried to do it myself and I still can't. I would like to say it's not the way my mind works but I know that would be wrong. Mind seems to be more a quality without any sense of dimension. Our limits are entirely self-imposed. We are locked in a box of our own creation—self-chosen limits. We can escape if we find the key. Unfortunately, the key lies in ways of thinking that are, by definition, outside the box.*

Don't delude yourself that this makes you special. Some of us have pushed our minds further, or been pushed as the case may be, but we are no better or different than anybody else. Each of us seems to have our own strength or ability but all of them are inherent in the nature of mind as a quality. The way we choose to structure our individuality determines how our abilities express themselves. Unconsciously we choose our limitations and what we are comfortable with. Most people are simply not willing or capable of giving up their grip on what they see as reality to chance living something better or different. For all of us, the fear of what might lie outside all our defenses is so enormous, paralyzing, that only the most extreme pressures break us out of them.

Argus's thoughts continued.

You had to be willing to change the way you see the world to be able to do what you did and making the choice is vital. It is part of the process. You decided William's fate. Hank suggested you probably could save William in a number of ways, but it was still up to you and whether you wanted it enough. He suggested both your and William's talents have not developed yet, though it is clear what some of them are regardless of that. When you and William have grown strong together, when you have created what you need to here, come for us. We will be waiting.

Awareness of his mind winked out as if it had never been there. It was so sudden it felt like a vacuum imploded.

William was right. I know now why it was so important I experienced William's journey directly, as he had experienced it. I have changed so much, come further than I ever thought possible partly because I lived through rather than heard about William's experiences. The paradox is, oddly enough, that I can now see clearly what I am has not changed at all. I am simply a little more aware of what I can be, what I really am, what you are, too.

I looked down to where William was still sprawled on the side of the road. I desperately wanted to run to him, but that would take too long, straight is best after all. Almost instinctively I plumbed the forces that appeared to hold me in their grip.

I stepped off the edge of the lookout into thin air because I knew I could.

In quietness and in confidence shall be your strength

ACKNOWLEDGEMENTS

I would like to acknowledge the commitment and dedication of my sensei, Johan Buiter, and that of the many other instructors who have taught me.

Thanks to my friends and dojo members who read, edited and commented on *William* for me.